ELVES' BELLS

A Ruby True Magical Mystery 2

NOVA NELSON

Contents

ELVES' BELLS

A Ruby True Magical Mystery 2

NOVA NELSON

Chapter One

The clock on the wall of the tearoom had hardly passed eleven, and Fifth Wind witch Ruby True's morning had already involved banishing two spirits. For a Tuesday, that seemed a little much, so she hardly blamed herself for being cranky. And the fact that Zax Banderfield had been scheduled to meet her five minutes ago and still hadn't arrived wasn't elevating her mood, either.

The West Wind witch Harvey Hardtimes, owner of A New Leaf where Ruby now waited, caught her eye from behind the counter. He raised his chin inquisitively as he held up a piping kettle. Her initial impulse was to wave him off, but, sure, why not have a fresh pot? She nodded as pleasantly as she could muster within the bounds of her mood.

The man had a few decades on her, and while she by no means considered him a father—anyone who'd met her own wretched father would understand why that might be considered an insult—Harvey was definitely fatherly in the traditional sense. But he was also rather motherly in that he had a nurturing nature about him she liked, if not loved.

Perhaps that was simply a result of him being a West Wind witch—one of the terramancers' innate strengths was being able to anticipate the needs of others and know how to fulfill those needs.

And surely it didn't hurt his desire to take good care of her that he made quite a bit of money off of her regular visits.

Ruby wondered unproductively what it would feel like to be a West Wind witch. Would she be in moods like this less often? What about if she were a North Wind witch, her head chronically in the clouds, paying no mind to who did and didn't show up for tea dates? Or a South Wind witch, a bold defender of the vulnerable, who wouldn't allow herself to sit here quietly when she could march right up to Fluke Mountain and call him out on his rudeness? Or perhaps an East Wind witch...

No, being stood-up would bother her even more if she were an East Wind witch with their desire for approval and strict adhesion to social conventions.

But in the end, it didn't really matter what it would be like if she were anything else, because she was a Fifth Wind, an enigma to the world, terrifying to some, and in times like these, indecipherable on the surface while roiling just below it.

Boy, she *was* in a mood. She decided to blame the annoying spirits for it and move on.

Along with the kettle and a fresh infuser of her favorite tea blend, Harvey brought over a small meat pie. She didn't care much for the pastry, but it wasn't for her. It was Clifford's special treat.

To the average observer, Ruby's familiar, a giant red hellhound, might have appeared asleep. And perhaps Clifford had been somewhere in that twilight realm, but his nose never took a break.

As the savory aroma of the hot pie had moved closer, he'd smacked his jowls and raised his shaggy head. And as Clifford's nose zeroed in on the scent, it also became more pronounced to Ruby, and she almost wished Harvey *had* grabbed one for her as well.

But she would have had to pay for that, and Cliff's was always on the house. That was just how it went with the hellhound. Most people in the little town of Eastwind never got past their initial terror of seeing a hellhound outside of the Deadwoods. But those who did and got to know the scruffy guy always had a soft spot for him. And that earned him some of the best food in town, at no charge to her.

As Harvey set down Ruby's refreshments, he said, "Waiting on a client?"

It was a harmless question, of course. This was where she usually met her potential clients, those unlucky enough to have one ghost too many in their lives, or who at least believed they did. Oftentimes the books falling off the shelves or missing keys had more to do with having children or cats in the home and less to do with a spirit from the beyond.

Hence her non-refundable consultation fee. She may spend a lot of time in spiritual realms, but she was still a down-to-earth business woman.

But today she wasn't waiting on a client. She was waiting on a handsome werebear. She was waiting on her *date.* And so the question of who she was expecting merely reactivated her grouchiness.

"No. I'm waiting on a friend. Or I was. I might stop waiting on him and start heading to the library for a few new reads."

Harvey nodded and presented her with a sympathetic frown. "If he's a no show, at least you can take heart that he's a fool. Any man who'd stand you up clearly doesn't have the sense to keep up with you anyway."

Ruby chuckled, pleased at how much the compliment improved her mood. "I'm sure he has a good excuse. He has a whole sleuth of werebears to look after, and you know how much trouble they can get themselves into."

Harvey's eyes narrowed. "Zax Banderfield? Is *that* who you're waiting on?"

"It... was."

He nodded. "He's a good one, I'd have expected better of him than leaving a lady waiting. Can I do anything to cheer you?"

She nodded toward he kettle. "I think this will do fine. Thank you."

Clifford finished the last crumbs of the pie, smacked his lips, and then laid his head back down again.

Just as Harvey made for the counter again, the familiar ring of a mail bell sounded outside the entrance to the tearoom to announce a new message. Through the front window, Ruby spied a spotted owl ruffle its feathers as it settled in on the perch above where it'd just dropped the letter.

The proprietor adjusted his trajectory to go retrieve the correspondence.

In her old life, back before she'd died and woke up in Eastwind, Ruby had heard that every time a bell rang, an angel got its wings.

However, now she knew better, considering she was friends with the town's only angel.

Ruby watched as Harvey took the slip of parchment from the delivery owl's claw and unrolled it. He frowned for only a second and then headed back inside, making straight for Ruby's table.

"It's for you."

Her Insight perked up and she knew even before reading it what it would say.

However, seeing the apology and explanation in Zax's own handwriting was somewhat comforting. Amid his busy schedule—the same one that apparently prevented him from keeping this commitment—he had taken the time to sit and write this.

That was something, she supposed.

She sighed and rolled up the letter, making an effort to smile at Harvey to demonstrate that she wasn't heartbroken.

Only once he left her did she have a moment to consider whether she *was* actually heartbroken. No, that seemed dramatic. She enjoyed Zax's company, and the two of them had been seeing more of each other over the last couple of months, but this was by no means the first time their work had interfered with their time together. And when one found meaning in one's work, like both she and the head of the werebear sleuth did, then that came first.

"He should have sent word earlier," Clifford said through their psychic connection.

"Maybe he did and the owl was slow."

Clifford grunted his skepticism.

Thankfully, Ruby was never without a book, and she reached in her large cloth bag and pulled out her current read in progress, *The Potent Prince.* She only had a few pages left in the epilogue of this one. The prince and his love, having finally overcome the many malevolent obstacles keeping them apart, were ready to consummate their marriage.

In other words, it was the best part of the book, and while she hadn't planned to enjoy it in a public place, she did find a thrill in the idea. No one need know what the red-haired, middle-age, Fifth Wind witch in her head-to-toe black garb was reading. If anyone asked why she looked flushed, she'd simply attribute it those pesky shifting hormones. That would teach them for prying. And then she would continue reading.

She made sure to firmly shut off her connection with Clifford before diving in—she'd forgotten to do that in the past, and little mental images had slipped through, causing him to growl at her until she snapped out of it and was able to keep her sordid thoughts to herself.

But just as she was thoroughly losing herself in the story, three noisy witches entered the tearoom like a tidal wave of nonsense. Their high-pitched voices were as pleasant as tambourines right next to her ears as they prattled on about the latest Coven gossip.

While she did love a solid bit of gossip, especially if it reinforced her own feelings about those in charge of the town, now was not the time.

She tried again to focus on her reading, but when they settled at the table right next to hers, she muttered, "Oh for fang's sake," marked her page with a thin ribbon, and then shut the book.

Her day was not getting any *less* obnoxious. It was almost as if Mother Earth and the Goddess Above had conspired to test her, to see how far she could be pushed before...

Before what, she wondered. What was the worst she could do?

"Raise the dead," Clifford supplied.

She'd let her mental barrier slip, but that was fine now that she wasn't reading any longer.

"True. Raising the dead is unpleasant business." She'd done it once before in her earlier years in town, back when she hadn't yet refined or fully explored her powers. The whole thing had been an accident, and she'd done her best to make amends with the family of the deceased whose expensive funeral she'd unequivocally ruined by carelessly letting her mind wander into the body of their grandmother without realizing it. It was only when she'd realized that *she* was the reason Grandma had jumped out of the casket and begun tap-dancing down the aisles of mourners that Ruby was able to rip her consciousness free.

Unfortunately, the dead collapsing in the middle of a dance routine was only slightly less traumatic for the onlooking children than when she'd jumped out of her supposed final resting place to begin with.

From the table over, one of the three witches cackled, and the noise put Ruby on edge. Plenty of people cackled, but when a witch did it, it just seemed so... stereotypical.

"I tell you, Gladys," said the witch, who by the look of her brown dress was a West Wind, "it's quite the revitalization! This could be huge for Eastwind. Tourism from Avalon has been on a decline over the last decade, but a vivacious art scene could be just the thing to breathe new life into it."

The witch who was presumably Gladys said, "If it were quality art, sure. But that's hardly what I would call the theater troops who have passed through so far."

"At the present, sure," said the third witch, whose red robes hinted that she might be a South Wind, "but it's a work in progress, so to speak. Every creative movement starts off somewhat crude and has to go through many iterations to become refined."

"Even still," said Gladys, "the number of iterations necessary to turn the local productions into true art, well, it could be decades, perhaps even centuries."

Ruby snickered into her teacup. Gladys and she might be on the same page regarding Eastwind's supposedly blossoming theater scene.

The South Wind said, "Oh, it's not so bad as that. I just caught a one-witch show the other day that was quite good."

Gladys conceded the possibility with a nod. "Logically speaking, if every actor in town is horrendous at the job, then a show with fewer actors *would* be a better show."

While the other two witches hemmed and hawed about that, Ruby grinned and even imagined befriending Gladys someday.

Local theater had become a scourge on the town over the last few months. It had started when a group of the wealthier Coven members had decided that Eastwind lacked culture. It may have even been one of the witches at the table next to her who had spearheaded that crazy notion. And the proposed solution was even crazier: build a stage in the Eastwind Emporium, the marketplace in the heart of town.

Whatever the original inspiration for the placement, the result was that at various points throughout the day, one could no longer go about one's shopping without the actors' grandiose voices, magically amplified, assaulting one's thoughts with whatever rubbish they so chose to recite.

Ruby couldn't stand it. A quiet town was a happy town, as far as she was concerned. Adding noise that no one asked for was a public nuisance. Ever since a team of leprechauns began assembling the stage, she'd secretly dreamed about a South Wind witch losing his or her temper and setting fire to it once and for all. If pyromancy had been within her skillset instead of necromancy, she would have already done it, perhaps disguised it as a somewhat powerful sneeze that got the best of her.

It surprised her to think that anyone might actually *enjoy* the performances on that stage. Mostly, when she'd been unfortunate enough to time her errands with one of the halfhearted productions, the small audience wore expressions of puzzlement. It was as if each person were trying to unlock the riddle of why in Earth's sake a group of adults would dress in silly costumes and parade around on what was little more than a wooden platform with musty curtains, reciting lines no one in their right mind would ever say. Or perhaps the transfixed audience was simply trying to figure out why anyone would expect to be *paid* for such a thing.

At least those were the questions Ruby had about it all. She didn't mind the occasional play back in her old world, but Gladys wasn't kidding when she said the level of talent in the Emporium had room for improvement.

As if reading her mind, the West Wind witch said, "Oh, but I heard today's performance will be quite something! The players have come all the way from Fallia and are known throughout the most refined realms!"

The South Wind clapped her hands excitedly. "We should definitely see it! What time does it start?"

"Eleven fifty, if I remember right," replied the West Wind. "But according to the flyer I saw for it over at the Pixie Mixie, they'll be in town for a week. So if we miss it today, we could catch one of the other shows."

Ruby looked up at the giant clock on the wall behind the counter. With a start, she realized it was just past eleven thirty.

If she was to finish today's errands in the Emporium before the play started, she needed to get a move on.

"Up, up, up!" she said to Clifford, who took his time getting to his feet. She needed a fresh cut of beef, a pound of potatoes, and a bunch of carrots if she was going to have what she needed for the stew she planned for supper, and the butcher was on the opposite side of the Emporium as her favorite vegetable cart. Oh! And she needed rosemary, too. Ruby'd almost forgotten that her neighbor Lilian's feline familiar had decided her rosemary bush was his new toilet and had urinated and clawed at the poor thing until it finally gave out and shriveled up. It would be back the next year—rosemary had its own way of rising from the dead—and she'd be sure to lay out some cat-repelling charms around it when that time came. But for now, she was forced to buy her rosemary. How humiliating.

And Lilian hadn't even apologized.

She waved goodbye to Harvey, left the appropriate coins on the table, and hurried out of A New Leaf and into the bright sunshine, praying—or as close to it as she ever came—that she could be safely back home before the first monologue.

Unfortunately for her, hardly a moment after the side street opened up into the bustling marketplace, she ran into the last person she wanted to see.

Chapter Two

... Or maybe he was the first person she wanted to see. The jury was perpetually hung on that matter.

Floating next to Ezra Ares were canvas bags overflowing with a mishmash of objects—stones, berries, ribbons, and even a few draw-string satchels that wriggled anxiously. The moment the South Wind's eyes found Ruby's, he broke into a wide grin, the same one that could sell matches to a dragon and kept business booming at Ezra's Magical Outfitters.

And the same grin that hadn't aged a day in over a decade.

While most witches preferred to wear the colors of their kind, Ezra almost never donned the fiery colors of the South Wind, instead opting for attire that complimented the rich, chocolate tones of his skin. Today, he was dressed nearly head to toe in a beautiful lilac suit with small bits of ornate orange embroidery around the collar and wrists. Perhaps that was his tip of the hat to his pyromancy, or perhaps he just thought it looked good on him.

And Ruby wouldn't have disagreed with that assessment. Her stomach twisted every time she saw him, regardless of what he was wearing.

Or not wearing.

Clifford nipped her on the hamstring. Whoops. Must have let that thought slip through. She'd been doing a lot more of that lately. Was her mind going already? Mid-forties seemed a bit early to start worrying about that.

Regardless, the small nip allowed her to get her mind out of the gutter and act like a completely normal witch (who could see and talk to ghosts), one who was not at all hung up on her un-aging ex.

"Well, if it isn't Ruby True! And just when I thought my day couldn't get any more fruitful."

"You've got quite a haul there," she said, nodding at his hovering bags.

"You're telling me! I came down here for one thing, and ended up with all this."

"What'd you come down here for?"

"Cactus flower."

She scanned his bags for such an item just as he groaned. "Of course. I forgot to buy the cactus flower. I got distracted over at Ogleman's booth by a lovely pair of binding stones he'd brought back with him from a trip to Zatrian and completely forgot about the one thing I needed."

"Don't be too hard on yourself. Distractions are easy to come by in the Emporium."

He did a quick scan of her. "I'd say."

She rolled her eyes and bit back a girlish grin. "Oh,

don't you start. I'm actually in a hurry myself. Need to get out of here before the performance starts." She nodded over to the stage where a handful of fairies already fluttered around, setting up the props and adjusting the curtains.

"I've heard this one is actually good," he said.

"How would anyone know that? They haven't performed yet."

"You know I have connections in other realms. Their reputation precedes them."

She bit back a snide remark.

"Anyway," he said, clearly sensing her sudden hostility, "you might consider sticking around and enjoying the entertainment if you don't have more pressing matters."

"Hmm..." she said, "I wish I could. But I *do* have more pressing matters. Namely, I have a comfortable chair by a quiet fireplace and the epilogue of a good book to finish."

"Would this comfortable chair be the same one I gave you?"

Ruby blinked. She'd forgotten about that. "Yes. Yes, it would."

She didn't appreciate his smug expression as he said, "Then I don't blame you. It wasn't a cheap purchase, but I knew the moment I saw it that it was made for you. Not sure I've ever made a better purchase."

She nodded at his current haul. "Keep this up, and the odds favor you eventually making one." Something lurched in the bottom of one of the sacks, as if trying to escape.

He laughed. "It's always a pleasure to see you, Ruby.

If you ever have a spare moment in your busy schedule, please come by the shop to say hello."

She arched a skeptical eyebrow. "Now, Ezra, I'd be a fool to willingly expose myself to your charms."

"And I'd be a fool not to keep trying to convince you." One last wink, and he had disappeared through the crowd, no doubt returning to Ogleman's booth to grab the cactus flower.

That was fine, she'd just avoid that area of the Emporium. She didn't need any of Olgeman's strange wares anyway. Her shopping list was much more mundane.

She glanced up at the ancient clock tower jutting out of the crowd clear across the Emporium. Eleven forty-five. "Siren's song," she cursed, shaking her head to clear it of the last encounter. Five minutes to gather everything she needed. She signaled to Clifford and they hurried toward the butcher shop.

Once she had her meat and potatoes and was waiting in line at Thaddeus Whirligig's herb cart, another familiar voice said hello. She turned and was pleasantly surprised to see Liberty Freeman standing behind her in line. "Liberty! How are you?"

The genie grinned. He was a sight to behold with his golden skin, and ivory smile. His muscles strained against the cream-colored linen of his shirt, and part of her wanted to tell him to just take the blasted thing off. He was the only genie she'd ever met, and she often wondered if all of them kept their biceps as bulky as an ogre's waist, or if Liberty had simply won the physical lottery. Although, with the overwhelming strength of magic each genie possessed, why wouldn't you give yourself every physical advantage possible?

All appearance aside, the genie was also the most personable member of the High Council and had clearly taken pains to learn the names of as many Eastwinders as possible. Above all his other qualities, she admired that aspect of him.

"Fantastic as usual, Ruby. Lovely day, isn't it?"

She hadn't noticed but nodded along anyway, keenly aware of how the genie's contagious charisma made every day seem a little bit brighter and teeming with possibility.

"Are you staying for the show?" he asked. "I heard the talent is unrivaled in all the connecting realms. Apparently, this troop won quite a few awards in Avalon."

Ruby didn't hold much stock in what the pretentious metropolitan realm of Avalon considered quality, but she decided to be pleasant anyway. "Unfortunately, I need to get back and start my stew for tonight."

It was a weak excuse, considering it wasn't yet noon, but Liberty didn't push. "That's too bad. Maybe you can catch one of the other shows later this week."

Just then, a rich and deep female voice blanketed the crowd. "Ladies and gentleman and all the rest, we humble request the honor of your attention..."

The play had started. Ruby gritted her teeth, and Liberty straightened up to see above the heads of the crowd, which he no doubt succeeded at, being at least a foot taller (and a foot broader at the chest) than anyone else in town.

Ruby bounced impatiently on her toes, waiting for the pixie in line in front of her to rattle off her full list to

Thaddeus. Finally, the druid had gathered all of her things and the pixie paid out and left, allowing Ruby to grab a few sprigs of rosemary and hurry toward home.

Clifford did her the favor of leading the way, as people were much more likely to step aside for a giant hellhound than for a petite Fifth Wind.

Not to say that she didn't hold her own intimidation factor around town. Those who hadn't put in the effort to get to know her avoided her like the plague. It was just one of the side effects of being able to speak to the dead.

She was nearly to the giant clock tower where the crowd thinned out considerably when she noticed another figure dressed much like herself: head to toe in black.

She waved to Ted, the town's grim reaper, who waved back overenthusiastically.

"Not staying for the show?" he said.

"No," she replied, drawing closer. "Afraid I have some, um, work to get to."

He nodded gravely. "I get it. I'm here on work, too."

Her eyes shot open. Ted only had one job, and no one wanted to be on the receiving end of it. "Oh, I see. In that case, I hope you won't find it rude if I put as much distance between us as possible."

He waved her off playfully. "Not rude at all. I'd hate to find out I'm here for you, anyway."

"That's very kind of you to say, Ted."

Suddenly, the bells in the tower above her boomed into life, swinging into the familiar tune they played before chiming the hour. The sound of them cut off any hope of continuing the conversation, which was just fine with her, and she jabbed the toe of her boot into Clifford's rear to spur him on.

The two of them hurried out and away from the Emporium as the clock began its dozen deep gongs to mark noon.

The clock had long fallen silent again by the time she reached her porch, blocks away from the market.

And it was in that silence that a sudden strong gust of wind carried to her ears screams from the direction of the Emporium.

Either the play was as good as everyone made it out to be, or Ted's work of clearing dead bodies was about to begin.

Chapter Three

Sheriff Gabby Bloom didn't usually bemoan getting out of her office and spreading her wings (literally). But when the situation was one like this, where she was delivering some unfortunate news to a friend, she often wished she could have just sent Deputy Titterfield instead.

Of course she wouldn't, though. For one, delivering the news herself was the right thing to do. It showed respect.

But mostly, she couldn't let the deputy know that she was about to give a heads up to a prime suspect.

She climbed the few stairs up onto the blue wooden porch of Ruby True's home, stomped her boots on the welcome mat a few times to rid them of their usual debris, and knocked. She made sure her fist made firm contact with the door four times. Four was an inherently angelic number and Bloom's standard for announcing herself, but that wasn't the only reason she made sure to count it out as she knocked on the Fifth Wind's door. Heaven help her if she ever fell short and knocked three times.

She'd once witnessed a delivery boy do just that and Ruby's red hair just about spontaneously combusted as she chewed him out for announcing himself in the manner of demons and other dark entities.

"Oh, hello," Ruby said, pulling open the door and staring through the threshold up at the sheriff. "I suppose I'm in trouble."

"You don't know that," said Bloom.

"I do. Either I'm in trouble, or you're in trouble and need my help, in which case I'm in trouble. Likely dire trouble at that."

"Fine," said Bloom. "You're in trouble. Now will you let me come in or would you rather the whole neighborhood and soon enough the whole of Eastwind know that I'm paying a visit to you immediately following a suspicious death?"

To Bloom's surprise, Ruby pursed her lips and seemed to consider it, staring up at empty space above the angel's head. "Depends. So long as I'm not arrested for it, that degree of suspicion *could* get people to leave me alone more often."

"I didn't mean for it to be a difficult decision."

"Oh, fine. Come in. I'm making dinner, and there's plenty to share."

Bloom stepped in past her. "Is that a bribe, Ms. True?"

"Absolutely."

Ruby shut the door, and Bloom couldn't help but smile as she entered the familiar, quaint space of the Fifth Wind's home. What Ruby referred to as the parlor was hardly more than a round wooden table with four chairs in the center of a large room that hosted a reading corner by a fireplace (where the witch's familiar was currently snoozing) and a kitchen complete with sink, stove, and cupboards. Bookshelves lined most of the walls, and a few small side tables holding strange objects Bloom didn't bother asking about filled the remaining space.

Nowhere were there any pictures of loved ones. Bloom had never noticed that before, and as soon as she did, it made her ache for Ruby's lonesome life. The only Fifth Wind in town, no husband or wife, no children, not even a small but close-knit group of friends...

But then Bloom remembered that she didn't have any pictures in her home or office either. And she remembered that she was the only one of her kind in town, too. And thank goddess for it.

The savory scent of stewed beef only added to the cozy feel of the place, and as Ruby shuffled back over to the stove, Bloom followed her in the direction of the scent. When Ruby lifted the lid, Bloom leaned over her, inspecting the contents.

Ruby elbowed her to get some space. "You'll get plenty, don't worry. Now go sit down, you're crowding me!"

Bloom grunted but agreed, and as she made her way over, she did her best to resist the urge to crouch—the warding baubles and totems hanging from the ceiling weren't *quite* low enough to risk hitting her head on them, but they were close.

Ruby banged a wooden spoon on the edge of the cast-iron pot after a good stir, and the sound caused Clifford's head to shoot up. With his eyelids remaining at half-mast, his nose twitched frenetically. His gaze fell briefly to

Bloom, who nodded respectfully at him. She thought he nodded back, but she couldn't be sure. A moment later, his head was down on his paws again and his eyes were closed.

Ruby brought over two bowls, set one on the ground in front of Clifford, saying, "It's hot, don't scald your tongue!" and then served the other to Bloom before returning to portion out one for herself.

As she settled in, Ruby said, "I suppose you ought to tell me what's going on. You said something about murder."

Bloom couldn't resist sampling the broth, and the small sip she managed scalded her tongue. She did her best to hide it as her eyes threatened to water, then she cleared her throat. "Suspicious death, not murder."

"Anyone I know?"

Bloom searched for a connection between the two, just like she'd done the moment she'd seen the victim's shirt, but she couldn't come up with one. And that boded well for Ruby. "Probably not. It was Bron Danann. An elf."

Ruby crinkled her nose and tapped a finger to her lips. "Nope, I don't believe I've heard of him. Or her?"

"It's a him. And I'm not surprised you haven't heard of him. He didn't leave Tearnanock Estates if he could help it."

A crease formed between Ruby's brows. "Tearnanock? I haven't heard of it. Is that in Eastwind?"

Bloom risked another sip, this time after blowing on the broth. She had to shut her eyes against the seductive taste. How had she ever carried on in Heaven without eating? Food had been vilified up there as a crutch for the weak and mortal. If that was truly the case, she was as weak and mortal as anyone. She dabbed her mouth with a cloth napkin from the table and said, "Yes, it's in Eastwind. But there's no reason you would be familiar with it. It's guarded by security measures. And it's invisible."

"Invisible?"

"Silly, I know. But the elves prefer it."

"I don't think I understand. There's an invisible part of Eastwind?"

Bloom chuckled. She enjoyed seeing Ruby caught unaware. Thanks to the psychic's Insight, she was usually a step ahead of Bloom, not behind. "There's more than one invisible part of Eastwind. I don't bother with those regions, though. If you don't want to be seen by anyone, including law enforcement, you forfeit your right to my protection. Of course, once they enter the visible realm, they're under my watch."

"So, Tearnanock Estates is invisible?"

"Right. It's a neighborhood nestled above Erin Park."

Ruby's eyebrows were at risk of disappearing beneath her shock of red hair. "Above?"

"Yes. You know Green Gale Avenue?"

Ruby nodded.

"Along both sides of the street, there's a second story, sort of like a platform that goes above it. All invisible. Mansions, green lawns, the works. That's Tearnanock. All elves."

"Too good for Erin Park?"

"They seem to think so. Granted, there are plenty of elves who live in Erin Park, but that's either because they don't approve of the segregation or because they simply can't afford it."

Ruby sipped her stew contemplatively, and Bloom took it as an opportunity to sample her first bite of beef.

The moment she bit down on it, she had to order herself not to moan.

After a moment of silence tainted only by the wet sounds of Clifford obsessively licking his bowl, Ruby said, "Is... is this a known fact?"

"Is what a known fact?"

"That Tearnanock exists."

"Not generally, no. It's more of a need-to-know basis. I'd appreciate it if you didn't share. So would the elves."

Ruby nodded slowly. "I have so many questions."

"So do I, but not about the invisible neighborhood. There's a dead guy, remember?"

Ruby blinked, nodded promptly, and straightened her posture. "Correct. Go on. Tell me what happened."

While Bloom would have rather used her mouth to eat than to talk, it was definitely best if they got down to business. "There's a lot I still don't understand about it, so I'll do my best. Deputy Titterfield was called to the Emporium at about ten after twelve today, right after Bron's body was discovered facedown on the cobblestones beneath the clock tower."

Ruby cringed as she spooned a bite of the stew into her mouth, and Bloom was sure that had nothing to do with the taste. The Fifth Wind dabbed her mouth with a napkin then said, "I presume it was best that he was facedown."

"You presume correctly. Thankfully, no one turned

him over to see the worst of the damage. At least not until Titterfield arrived."

Morris Titterfield was a fine deputy. But he was getting up there in years and had become somewhat callous after the repeated exposure to violence and death. And sometimes he forgot that the general public wasn't. "He flipped Bron over to check for vitals, but of course the elf had none."

"The clock tower is tall."

"Exactly. And I believe your line of thinking is correct. It seems that Bron jumped from the top of the tower."

"Or," Ruby suggested, "someone pushed him."

The sheriff nodded. "And that's why it's a suspicious death. Titterfield spoke with a few of those in the area who were familiar with the deceased, and no one had any idea why Bron would jump. No signs of that sort of thing. He lived a happy life, by all accounts."

"But then again," Ruby said, "the deputy was asking people before the body was even removed from the scene."

Bloom held up a hand to stop her. "I know, I know. The odds of hearing anything else right after his death are slim. But if he *did* do it himself, I would have expected *someone* to say something to the effect of 'I saw this coming and no one believed me.' And Titterfield didn't report anything like that. People don't like to speak ill of the dead, but they sure as Heaven like being proved right."

Ruby nodded. "Good point. Being right is the best." She paused, and Bloom recognized that look of deep consideration well enough to avoid interrupting it. Best to give Ruby's mysterious mind room to wander.

"So Titterfield turned the elf over, presumably revealing grisly injuries from the impact. That's macabre enough. But why are *you* here? Naturally, you would want to know if I heard anything from the deceased, but you could have sent that in a letter. And yet, here you are, eating my food and describing death. I must be a suspect."

Bloom bit back a smile. "I do love the way your mind works. And yes, you're a suspect. Or you will be once word spreads of what else was found on the body."

Ruby sighed. "I take it you mean I'll be a suspect in the eyes of the public, but not yours."

"Correct. I don't think you did it because I know you, and I know that you don't have the energy to waste on something as petty as murder. Not to mention you lack motive, and Ted said he saw you leave the Emporium before the death occurred."

"You spoke with Ted?"

"Not me. Titterfield. Ted was the one who called it in. If he has any indication that a death involves foul play, he lets us know before hauling off the body. Due to the crime scene, you were an obvious suspect right off the bat, but Ted swore he saw you and Clifford leave before the death took place."

"Right. You keep hinting that there was something off about the crime scene. Care to enlighten me?"

This was the part Bloom had dreaded. Not because she thought it implicated Ruby, but because it would be difficult to keep everyone else from believing that, and the Fifth Wind would pick up on that right away, and surely not be thrilled.

"When the deputy rolled Mr. Danann over, we presume that the surrounding crowd were preoccupied with the sight of the unfortunate impact wounds. But it's possible that at least one person might have noticed the stains on the elf's white shirt. They weren't blood. As far as we can tell, they were berry stains. Someone had written in berry juice on his shirt prior to his fall."

Ruby's eyes had narrowed down to slits. "And? What did it say?"

Bloom inhaled deeply. "Titterfield couldn't make it out on scene, but I got a look at it back at the station. It clearly said *5th*."

Ruby's eyes shut slowly, and her head tilted back. Bloom could see her nostrils flare as she inhaled deeply. Finally, she exhaled and opened her eyes again. "I can see how that might implicate me. But I can also see how it might implicate Ed Willow, the berry vendor whose cart is right next to the clock tower."

"But everyone loves Ed." Bloom realized what she'd said too late and tried to scramble. "Not to say that nobody loves you. Just that, well, Ed is a bit of a town icon, you know? He's generous, young, handsome, and—"

"And I'm none of those things."

"I didn't say that."

"You said as much." Ruby dismissed it with a flick of her wrist. "But don't worry, you're not telling me anything I don't know. Ed is as fine a witch as they come. He's the quintessential West Wind, and who doesn't love them? A Fifth Wind, on the other hand..."

Bloom nodded gravely. "Right. That's all I meant.

You're at a disadvantage because of the preexisting stigma around your kind. And the fact that our only real clue is the words *5th* doesn't exactly help your case if it gets out."

"Let me get this straight." Ruby set down her spoon and folded her hands in her lap. "You came here not because this is a matter for a psychic to attend to, but because you wanted to tip off a possible suspect in your own case."

"That about sums it up."

Ruby grinned. "I knew you were a rebel."

Bloom chuckled. "Why do you think I'm down here and not up there?" She nodded toward Heaven. "But still, you should stay vigilant for a while. Bron Danann was a well regarded elf. He's been in Eastwind for hundreds of years. I don't know how the other elves will respond to it. The rest of Eastwind doesn't know him well, but they do love a reason to turn on someone they already fear."

"I never thought I'd say this, but I hope Bron's spirit *does* drop in for a word. Could be quite useful for my continued survival."

"I don't think there'll be a mob anytime soon. Also, we're a little bogged down at the department—"

"Nothing new there."

"You're not wrong. But if you don't have any more pressing matters and would be willing to help investigate this case, we'd be grateful."

"More pressing matters than proving I didn't push a well-respected elf off a tall building? I'll have to check my calendar, but no, I don't suspect I have anything more pressing at present."

"You've got the mind for this, Ruby. If I could ever get the High Council to loosen the purse strings of the Sheriff's Department budget just a little, I'd hire you on full-time."

"No, you would not. Because I'd never accept that job."

"Either way..." Bloom leaned over and pulled a gold coin from her back pocket, setting it on the table. "That's for your trouble. And the stew."

"I can't possibly take your money for this."

Bloom shrugged. "And I wouldn't possibly offer you my own money. This is from the evidence cavern."

Ruby's spine straightened in an instant. "The *evidence cavern?*"

"Yes, ma'am. The caves are filled with plenty of junk, but any money associated with illicit dealings ends up down there, too. We probably have more gold stashed away than there is in the treasury behind Rainbow Falls. Of course, it's temping to use it to supplement our paltry operating budget, but that large-scale use would be wrong. It might indirectly motivate me to seize more funds, perhaps even at the cost of true justice."

"But skimming a little off the top to pay a witch for her trouble is fine?"

"I don't see why not." Bloom winked.

"Your view of right and wrong both baffles and impresses me, Gabby."

"Then I suppose I'm doing something right."

Ruby chuckled. "Who has Deputy Titterfield spoken with already?"

"Just those on scene, as far as I'm aware. He'd already been on duty for nearly twenty hours by the time he cleaned up the scene and completed the initial interviews, so I sent him home to sleep. He's not as young as he used to be."

Ruby dismissed it with a wave of her hand. "None of us are. Oh. Well, maybe you."

Bloom shrugged a weak apology she didn't really feel. Ah, to be mortal. She'd dreamed of it. How invigorating life must be to know it had an end!

Meanwhile, the short-lifers envied her position. Perhaps the best spot was the one in the middle, to be a long-lived being like the elves.

Long lived until someone shoves you off a clock tower.

"One more question," Bloom said.

Ruby had just finished her stew and was drinking the broth straight from the bowl, which seemed a sensible thing to do with food as delectable as this. As she set it back on the table, she arched a single eyebrow. "Yes?"

"Got anything for dessert?"

Chapter Four

Ruby awoke the following morning after a night of uninterrupted sleep.

And that raised a few important questions. Because it meant the ghost of Bron Danann hadn't visited her.

Usually, if a spirit of the newly deceased was going to come knocking, it did so within a day or two of its death. There were exceptions, of course; spirits that wandered for years, decades, millennia, and finally stumbled upon her home by mere accident, only to be pleasantly surprised when someone acknowledged their presence. And then there were spirits who took to tormenting others the moment they materialized, and Ruby only ever saw those when the tormented individuals called her in.

There was still time for Bron to appear, but she suspected he wouldn't. She couldn't pinpoint why, but there it was. It must be her Insight determining that, since such was usually the case when she couldn't understand how she knew something.

Over the years of practicing her craft, she'd come to

believe that her so-called magical gift of Insight, while definitely a useful tool, wasn't all that magical. Instead, rather than being a sense all its own, it was simply a booster to her other senses. While her eyes looked at many things during the day, her conscious mind only retained a few of them, the ones that seemed most relevant to whatever she was doing at the time.

But in the background, her Insight was cataloguing everything. She might not notice a detail as small as a title on a stranger's bookshelf or a statue resembling an obscure deity, but her Insight did. And when she saw that book or statue again, and then again, in different locations during her investigation, that was when her gift would begin to poke at her to tell her to take notice.

Or sometimes the connections were even more abstract. Either way, her Insight paid attention to what her conscious mind often glossed over—scents, sounds, phrases, even behaviors.

She might have made a good detective if she didn't find playing by the rules so restrictive.

Ruby's knees and ankles crackled as she stood from bed and pulled her nightgown tightly around her. Was it normal for one's body to pop and clatter like this so young? Then again, middle age was a strange, unfathomable thing. Feelings of youth and old age took turns hitting her in waves, though she was definitely feeling the impact of the latter more keenly now, especially first thing in the morning. A good night's sleep didn't go as far as it used to.

By the time she had eaten breakfast, fed Cliff, and gathered her things, she had a good idea of where she would head first on the day's investigations.

Her thinking was this: interview those she personally knew first, because, in the event that word had gotten out about what was written on Bron's shirt, they would be less likely to suspect her without speaking to her directly. She was sure she could provide satisfactory explanation as to why she hadn't been involved in the suspicious death. So she would build herself a few allies first before moving forward.

And that was why, despite her better judgment and Clifford's questions about her true motivation, she left her home and made straight for Ezra's Magical Outfitters.

"I don't understand what you expect to get from this," Clifford said as he padded along next to her up the road toward the more expensive shopping district.

"He was at the Emporium, wasn't he? We saw him. And then he said he'd forgotten cactus flower, so he went back for it. He might have seen something."

"If he'd seen something, wouldn't he have mentioned it to Titterfield when he arrived?"

"Possibly. But it's equally likely that Ezra has remained tight lipped. With as much under-the-table business as he conducts, it wouldn't surprise me if he needed to pretend he was never there that day to keep clear of Bloom or Titterfield sniffing around."

It wasn't that Ezra was a crook. That word implied some sort of malignant spirit or deficiency. Ezra loved helping others by finding just the object they needed to improve their lives. What he didn't love was laws. Primarily, those regarding imports and exports. When the South Wind said he would get you whatever you needed, he wasn't just blowing smoke; he would locate it and get it to Eastwind, whether it was officially banned or not. Ruby had always found something terribly admirable in that.

And he did have his moral code. He'd once told her about a patron's request for flickerbark, which everyone knew could only be used for one thing: setting large fires to inflammable objects. That, he'd said, didn't seem like a great idea to deliver into anyone's hands... though he did know a guy in Avalon who could get him some, if it ever came to that.

Ruby strolled into the shop, but Clifford paused before the threshold. *"Do you need me?"*

She considered it, knowing the hound preferred the fresh air. *"I could benefit from your sharp mind, yes."*

He nodded and followed her in. What went unspoken was that sometimes Ruby's own sharp mind became a bit blunt when she was in close proximity to the flirtatious Ezra. But Clifford had enough tact not to mention it.

She paused just inside and took in the surroundings. Ezra's Magical Outfitters could get crowded at certain points of the year, especially as Halloween approached and everyone tried to ward themselves against the onslaught of spirits as best they could. But on a Wednesday morning in the middle of May, she spied only one other patron wandering the glass display cases toward the front of the store. She was a stunning elf with long copper hair, skin the color of lamb's milk, and emerald eyes. Ruby had a strange urge to ask her, "Do you live in Tearnanock Estates?" and then "Can you give me a tour?"

But before her poor judgment could get the best of her, Ezra appeared from behind one of the long wooden shelves at the back of the store, and his face lit up when he saw her. Today's ensemble included a loose-fitting violet shirt, brown slacks, and a string of red stones around his neck that Ruby guessed to be aventurine. He always did love that particular gem.

He hurried over, arms spread. "Ruby! To what do I owe this pleasure?"

The browsing elf looked up at that, blinked at Ruby a few times, and then seemed to make the connection. Not everyone had met her in person, but most everyone in town knew Ruby True by reputation. And she was left to conclude *that* was why the elf quickly hugged her purse to her and scurried out without another word.

Ruby watched the elf go, and once the door shut behind her, the Fifth Wind felt more able to speak freely. "I assume you've heard about what happened at the Emporium yesterday."

Ezra pulled up short, his arms falling limp by his sides. "Yes, I did. So unfortunate. Did you know him?"

"Not at all." She paused. "Do you know about Tearnanock Estates?"

He tilted his head to the side. "Yes, what about it?"

"You know it exists?"

"Of course."

She grunted. "And have you ever been there?"

Now a wide grin washed away the signs of his confusion. "Oh yes! It's wonderful. Does this have something to do with the elf's death?"

Rather than tell him the truth, that it didn't have much to do with the investigation but plenty to do with her feeling bitter she'd somehow lived seventeen years in this town without knowing about an invisible avenue not far off the main circle, she said, "It's where the deceased resided."

He nodded solemnly. "Then I imagine they're having a spectacular funeral for him up there soon. Maybe even as we speak." He shook his head. "Man, I wish I could see it. They really do things up in Tearnanock."

"That seems a little insensitive," she chided. "But back to the task at hand. Did you happen to see anything suspicious while you were in the Emporium? Titterfield and Bloom are so far stumped."

He crossed his arms over his chest and frowned. "That's never a good sign. I mean, Titterfield isn't as keen as he used to be, but Bloom is sharp as a vampire's fangs."

"True. But she's also overworked."

Ezra nodded. "What does the elf's ghost have to say? I assume he's come back to visit you, or else why would you be here?"

"He hasn't visited me. Perhaps he will—some take time adjusting to their new existence. But if I'm going to see him at all, he should appear by midday tomorrow."

"He's clearly not a smart ghost," Ezra said.

Ruby tilted her head, narrowing her eyes at him. "Why do you say that?"

"No smart man would keep you waiting." He winked.

Ruby pressed her lips together to avoid betraying herself with a smile. If Ezra wanted to flirt, he would have to do better than that.

But wait. She *didn't* want him to flirt. Right. She'd almost forgotten. There would be no purpose in flirting now, as it'd lead nowhere, and likely only make her feel even worse once she left the store, stirring up memories of the days when they flirted freely and unabashedly nonstop. Days when the flirting could and *did* lead to something.

"Did you see the death occur or not?" The words came out much sharper than she'd intended.

Ezra didn't seem ruffled, though. "Afraid I didn't. I had my back to it, watching the play."

"How far were you from the clock?"

"Twenty-five feet, perhaps."

"Were you close to where the body landed then?"

"Startlingly close, but not the closest. It's a wonder he didn't land on someone."

Ruby had considered that, too. It was lucky that the theater hadn't drawn such a large crowd that the entire Emporium was packed all the way back to the clock. There could have been another casualty associated with this already messy business.

Would Bron Danann have jumped if there were people below? Or, given the other possible scenario, would someone still have pushed him?

"I hate to be morbid," Ruby said, "but my assumption is that there's a sound associated with a body falling from that distance."

"Ah," he said, wagging his finger playfully, "not so much the falling, but the landing."

She arched a brow. "You heard it, then?"

"Nope. Didn't hear a thing in that regard." He spread his hands, palms up, to demonstrate his ignorance. "I didn't know about it until I heard Ted ordering people to move. The play was between scenes, and his voice caught my attention. Then I saw the poor elf lying facedown."

"Did no one see the poor man fall?" Ruby asked, more to herself.

"It was an interesting play," Ezra replied. "Engrossing."

"Clearly."

After a moment's pause, Ezra said, "I never even saw who it was."

"It was Bron Danann."

Ezra sucked in air like he'd been punched. After a moment more, he exhaled, his shoulders appearing to deflate. "Ah, poor Bron."

"You knew him?"

"Not well, but yes. He came in occasionally, and I shared a drink with him once at Pan's Patio. You remember that old bar?"

Mother Moon, did she. And she remembered some of her times with Ezra there, back before it shut down for "forgetting" to pay taxes for one hundred and fifty years. But instead of indulging in the fond memories he was clearly trying to evoke with the question, she simply said, "I do."

Ezra continued, "It's too bad that place ended up burning to the ground."

"Did you have anything to do with that?"

"Oh *sure*," he said, "blame the pyromancer."

She shrugged a single defiant shoulder. "Why not? Everyone always blames the necromancer."

"True. But no, I actually had a dream of buying that place and reopening it. But it's hard to reopen a pile of ashes."

They fell silent for a moment, and Ruby momentarily forgot why she'd come in the first place.

"If he didn't see or hear anything, we should get a move on," Clifford prompted gently.

"Right." She straightened up but was still a few inches shorter than Ezra, who was not himself a tall witch. She offered him a professional nod. "I'd better get going. Many more people to talk with before we can put this mystery to bed."

She cringed at the mention of bed around him, but he didn't seem to notice.

"As always, Ruby, it's been a pleasure. Come back any time you want. I should be getting an order of gorgeous abalone shells and jet in the next couple of days, if you need to refresh your collection."

She did love a good abalone shell with its rainbow pearling. She must already have ten of them lying around her home to hold her various sage bundles. But an eleventh wouldn't hurt...

"If I need any of that, I know where to find you."

And then she turned and left the shop before she said or did anything further to humiliate herself.

Once she was certain she was out of sight of anyone in the shop, she paused underneath the shade of a large maple to absorb the facts so far. "If he didn't even know who it was, then it seems unlikely that he knew anything about the writing on the elf's shirt." She should have asked him about it directly, but once she had become flustered, all she'd been able to think about was wrapping up the conversation.

"Maybe that means word hasn't gotten out. Ezra's usually the first to hear that sort of thing."

"A girl can hope."

Clifford sat in the shade next to her, but even so, his

ears continued to twitch like radio dishes. *"Where to now, boss?"*

"A place we've never been before."

"That could be a lot of places." A fly buzzed around his muzzle, and in a flash, he struck, his teeth clicking together, and the offending pest was dead in his jaws.

"Are you calling me a shut in?"

He smacked his lips, clearly trying to locate the fly in his cavernous mouth. *"I plead the Fifth."*

"I never should have told you about the Constitution. I knew it would come back to bite me." She paused. "Wait."

"Oh." He stopped smacking. He'd just realized what he'd said, too. *"Do you think...?"*

"I don't see how it could relate. Elves are from Fallia. I doubt they share a Constitution with the United States."

"You're probably right. But still. It's the right kind of thinking. '5th' could refer to anything."

He had a point. She would have to keep her mind open, but in the meantime, she had more people to interview.

She'd sent a letter to her next interviewee earlier that morning, and the genie had cheerily agreed to speak with her, so long as she would make the trek to his house.

"You never answered my question," Clifford said. *"Where to next?"*

"The home of Liberty Freeman."

She didn't miss Clifford's tail wagging, and if she'd had one herself, it would have been wagging too.

Chapter Five

Ruby checked the address on Liberty's letter once more. Had he misprinted it? Surely this couldn't be his address, because it wasn't even a building.

She was sure she had followed his directions to the letter, though. And yet here she and Clifford were, standing in an open field on the edge of town, facing a single wooden door. No building behind it. Just the door.

It looked like someone had painted it gold years ago, but only a few curling strips of the paint still clung to the wood. She turned in a circle, looking around. Behind her, she could see the edge of the town proper. But between that and where she stood was easily a quarter mile of open field, slightly overgrown except for the footpath that led here, to this lonely door. On the other side of it, more grass, and perhaps fifty yards on, a dense tree line. Bright clumps of sunflowers dappled the land, but she had no mental energy to spare for their beauty.

She walked to the other side of the door. It looked just the same as the front

"I smell him all around here," said Clifford.

So perhaps Liberty had taken a note out of the elves' book and made himself an invisible home.

She trusted Clifford's nose more than she trusted what her eyes could see, so she said, "Either there's a great bit of magic involved, or I'm about to look like a complete fool." And then she stepped up to the door and knocked.

And then an even stranger thing happened. From the other side of the door—no, not the other side because that was just more grass—she heard Liberty's voice. "Come in. It's open."

She exchanged a glance with Cliff, and then she turned the old brass doorknob.

When her eyes adjusted to what was through the doorway, her first words were, "Oh, for fang's sake."

It was the stark contrast between the serene field and the lively scene that now stood ahead of her that had elicited the response.

But at the same time, *of course* Liberty Freeman lived in a tropical oasis. He was a magical genie. Why wouldn't he?

She'd never been to Las Vegas in her old world, but she'd seen pictures of the over-the-top hotels and casinos with sparkling interiors, replicas of classic art and sculpture, fountains that shot up toward the ceiling, and gold, gold, gold over everything. But those were all facades—plastic made to look like metal, gold-colored acrylic paint, and so forth. Meanwhile, she had a feeling that everything in Liberty's expansive property was the real deal.

Once Clifford was in, she shut the door, which, on

this side appeared to be a tall, ornately carved slab of marble. When she took a step back to get a better look at it, there was an entire scene depicted on its surface. It was too much to take in, but she could definitely make out Liberty himself standing at the center of the image, arms outspread, his riotous grin easily recognizable.

"*This is quite something,*" said the hellhound in his usual understatement.

"*Indeed.*"

Nothing about the dimensions of the space in which they now found themselves matched up to the one they'd just left, so Ruby let that expectation drop completely. Instead, she simply marveled at the foyer—was that even the right word for something this large?—in which they stood. Beneath their feet was a checkerboard pattern of violet and ivory marble tiles, and to either side ran long rectangular slabs of what looked like onyx, each with a steady wall of water shooting up from the center like little mohawks. But the mohawks kept her from seeing much beyond them to her left or right, so instead she focused her attention ahead, toward the enormous circular fountain that seemed to shoot tendrils of liquid gold rather than water. Or perhaps that was just the effect of the sun streaming down on it through the marvelous glass ceiling above it.

"No wonder he's always in a good mood," she mumbled to Clifford.

As they started forward, she jumped when a dolphin leaped up out of the fountain then plummeted gleefully back in.

Liberty had dolphins. Noted.

A curvaceous woman appeared around the end of

one of the long runner fountains. Her dark hair was pulled back in a tight top knot and the various layers of her teal silk dress clung to her sensually. "Welcome," she said. Her voice was deep and rich. "Liberty is expecting you in the tearoom."

Ruby found the idea of a tearoom done to this level of extravagance thrilling. Would it be *extra* cozy? How many flavors of tea would the genie have on hand? Ooh! Would he be able to match the perfect blend to her present mood? There was a whole branch of magic on that particular skillset, but she hadn't yet gotten around to studying it.

"My name is Ellysia," said the woman as she led them around the central fountain. She wore no shoes, simply padded barefoot, which she made seem like the most erotic way to walk. "If you need anything while you're visiting, simply say my name and I'll appear. No need to yell it. Simply say it with the intent of summoning me."

Ruby glanced down at her own feet and frowned. Her boots weren't what she would normally call dirty, but in this pristine environment, they looked like nothing short of a serious health hazard. "Should I, um, take my shoes off?"

"It's not necessary, but if that would make you more comfortable, I can assist you."

She imagined sitting on the edge of the fountain while Ellysia untied her boots and pulled them off like a mother would her child's. "No, thank you."

Behind the fountain lay two wide staircases branching off in different directions with a balcony connecting them on the second story. The railings resembled giant serpents with jewel-encrusted scales. And below the balcony, nestled between the staircases, was a long hallway sloping downward and out of sight. That was the route they took.

By the time Ellysia announced that they had arrived at the tearoom, Ruby had long forgotten why she'd even come. She'd seen so many marvelous things already that her mind was in another place. An elf falling from a clock tower seemed paltry and mundane by comparison.

"Welcome!" announced Liberty, as Ellysia held open the door for Ruby and Cliff.

He rose from a large wingback chair by a fire and approached with his arms open wide. Ruby hardly registered that, though, as she took in the tearoom. It *was* amazing!

But then her view of it was obscured as the genie wrapped her in his large, muscular arms, and her face pressed against his sternum.

"Mm-mm-mm!" he said, flexing with each grunt. Finally, he let her go, and she felt strangely exposed. She cleared her throat and patted her hair back into place as Liberty high-fived Clifford then gave him a few noggin scratches.

"Thank you, Ellysia," he said, and the voluptuous assistant nodded and shut the door behind them. "Come on in! I knew the moment you wrote that I absolutely had to show you this room. I said to myself, 'No one will appreciate it like Ruby True!' and if your expression tells the tale, I was right."

"It's... quite something," she said. But 'quite something' was both highly accurate and grossly inaccurate.

Unlike the brilliantly lit foyer, this room had low ceilings—not so low that Liberty was forced to crouch, but low enough to give the space a sheltered feeling. In fact, upon her further inspection, she discovered that the ceiling was the roof of a cave, though without any hazardous stalactites dangling from it.

She wouldn't let herself get hung up on that detail, though, because the rest of the room was equally, if not vastly more magnificent. Wingbacks and loveseats and day beds and even a papasan were scattered around at intervals, each with a perfectly shaped side table next to it that had multiple shelves built in to house however many books one might want to stash alongside them for the day's reading hours. And above each of these seats floated a small glowing orb, something she'd never encountered until Eastwind but had since grown quite used to. Each orb emitted enough soft light to read by, but not so much as to disrupt the dim and cozy feel of the space. The orbs reminded her of the fireflies she used to watch back in Illinois on hot summer days.

The room was of an irregular shape, with the walls curved like they were actually in a cave that had once held water to slowly wear its edges smooth with time. And perhaps that's exactly where they were. Eastwind was built over a spring anyway. But more than likely, the room was a result of the same magic Liberty had used to construct this entire luxury complex.

Along the walls were a series of custom bookshelves, each one bending to fit the curvature of the wall against which it stood.

It was a fantastic collection of books already, but what took it from good to great was that when Liberty pressed a flat palm against the edge of one, it rotated, and in its place another bookshelf of the same shape appeared. How exactly that worked within the dimensions of space Ruby was familiar with, she couldn't explain. But magic, as she understood it, worked in many more dimensions than the four she interacted with on a regular basis.

He pressed his palm to the shelf again, and it rotated once more. "Each one rotates a thousand and one times, if I fill it with that many books."

Ruby's eyebrows shot up. "Each one?" She did a quick estimate of the number of bookshelves and found it must be at least two dozen. If each one held around a hundred books...

The mental math was beyond her, but she knew it to be a very large number of books.

Liberty chuckled. "What else does one do in this town except work and read?"

She shook her head vaguely. "You're asking the wrong person if you expect an answer."

"I knew you'd appreciate this. One last thing: tea! And then you can ask me whatever you like."

He led her over to a small empty shelf, and with a snap of his fingers, a piping hot kettle appeared on a metal tray with two copper tea cups and one sausage, still sizzling. She knew who the latter was for.

A small metal tea box had also appeared on the shelf next to the tray, and Liberty nodded toward it. "Go ahead and open it. It should have the perfect blend for you in your present state all ready to go."

Her heart leaped in her chest. This was literally her dream come true.

For a moment, she wondered if a genie like Liberty could ever go for a witch like her. She and Clifford could certainly find a way to adjust to this life. And after all, she would be dead in less than fifty years, and what was half a century to an immortal being like Liberty? They wouldn't even need to be intimate. She could just live here and chat about books with him. Surely that would earn her keep.

"I don't show my house to many people because I worry that they'll start devising ways to never leave," Liberty said cheerfully.

Ruby's head snapped around to look at him. "Oh. That would just be... silly. The thought never even crossed my mind."

Had he read her thoughts? Could genie's do that? It was always hard to know what they could and couldn't do, since they were known to rarely show their hands, but it was a safe bet to just assume they could do anything. She'd have to be more disciplined with her imagination until she left.

She opened the metal tin and discovered not only a decadently fragrant teabag, but a tiny flask. She held it up to examine it in the low light. "What's in it?"

Liberty shrugged. "Whatever you need at the moment. Hey, don't worry. I'm not judging." He grinned.

"Well," she said, feeling a slight thrill run through her, "I would certainly hate to reject what I need at this moment." She unscrewed the top and sniffed it. She would recognize the sweet smell of bourbon anywhere.

She popped the teabag into her cup and set it and the flask on the tray. Once Liberty had also received his tea recommendation, they headed over to two wingback chairs by the fire. The tray floated along behind, landing gently on a small brass table between them without spilling a drop.

Once their tea was steeping, he crossed one leg over another and said, "What can I help you with, Ruby?"

"This tea is certainly a good start." Just the mere fumes of the alcohol burning off in the hot water were enough to make her feel quite good. "But I'm afraid I'm also here to see what you know of Bron Danann. Did you know him?"

The mention of the dead man didn't appear to dampen the genie's mood, and for the first time, it occurred to her that he might be intentionally distracting her with the dazzling display of his home. Did he know the effect it would have on her? Was that part of a scheme?

"I did," he admitted, "but not well. Very few people seemed to know him beyond acquaintanceship. He was friendly but mostly kept to himself. He moved to Eastwind a few hundred years ago with a small group of elves, and they kept each other's confidence."

"Any idea what he did for work?"

Liberty sipped his tea then said, "Nothing, as far as I know. He was wealthy. Perhaps he did something up on Tearnanock, trading or some such, but I don't visit there. I know this may appear a bit hypocritical coming from someone who lives in an invisible house, but I don't completely love the way the Tearnanock elves have shut themselves off from everyone else. Some view diversity as something to tolerate, but I truly believe that it makes for a healthier community. I assume most people who come from somewhat homogenous realms would agree."

Ruby thought of Gabby Bloom, who'd left Heaven just to escape the monotony of a bunch of smug angels. In the brief silence, she heard Clifford's slobbery jowls continue to smack, even though he'd undoubtedly finished off his treat mere seconds after she'd given it to him. "How did you know him?"

"I helped them get set up. Tearnanock Estates didn't exist when he and his friends came to Eastwind, so he moved into Erin Park. But when he heard about my set up"—he gestured broadly to the surroundings—"he got the idea in his head that he would like to live in an invisible home, too. And then some of his other elf friends thought that might be nice, too, and the idea spread, but only among the elves."

"Why only among the elves? Now that I know it's possible, I should like the same. No unwanted visitors."

"It didn't spread beyond the elves because the elves didn't tell anyone about it. Like I said, this group doesn't like to mix much with others. So I told them, fine, I'd help them set up an invisible avenue so long as they didn't tell anyone about it and *definitely* didn't tell people I was the one who made it possible." He shook his head. "If word got around, I'd be so pestered by everyone, I'd have to give up my seat on the High Council and go into invisible construction for the rest of eternity."

Ruby grinned. "Your secret's safe with me."

He waved her off. "Oh, I'm sure it is or I wouldn't have told you."

"But you should know that Ezra and the sheriff are also well aware of Tearnanock."

He leaned back in his chair and crossed his tree trunk legs. "The sheriff knows because I ran it by her first. And

Ezra knows because, well, of course he does. He has a nose for anything that could prove strategic for him." Liberty beamed. "I wouldn't be surprised if he already had a safe house somewhere up there, in case one of his dealings went wrong and he needed a place to lie low."

"You too?" Ruby asked.

Liberty arched an inquisitive brow.

"I just mean, everyone lets Ezra get away with things. And I understand when it comes to most people—he can supply them with what they can't get elsewhere. But you're a genie, for fang's sake! Can't you just snap your fingers and have all of this suddenly appear? You don't need Ezra's help."

Liberty listened intently, sipping his tea as he did. "You're right, I could technically create all of this on my own, but I have to hold the idea in my mind first. The rotating bookshelves, for instance. I can't create them if I can't *imagine* them. And Ezra has one of the best imaginations I've ever seen. When I first built this place, it was mostly empty. Very uninspiring. I would think up little things here and there and magic them into existence, but for hundreds of years it lacked the details you now see. When I met Ezra only a handful of decades ago, however, I surmised immediately that he had a mind for the ornate, so I enlisted his help. He assisted me in imagining up so much of the luxuries and intricacies. And so, yes, I turn a blind eye to whatever unlawful activities he might partake in, so long as they don't injure anyone else—Eastwind has far too many unenforceable or simply ridiculous and restrictive laws, you know. Besides, Ezra is simply a joy to be with."

She brought her own teacup to her lips to disguise the

small grunt of annoyance. Liberty wasn't wrong. Ezra *was* a joy to be with. And if she wanted sympathy for her situation, for how things had turned out between them, she was unlikely to get it from an immortal who similarly never aged.

"Back to Bron," she said. "You were in the Emporium when he died. Any chance you saw it happen?"

"If I had, I would have alerted Sheriff Bloom immediately. But I was busy watching the play. It was quite something. A historical tragedy—not generally my favorite as I enjoy a good bit of comedy in my entertainment, but it was good for what it was."

"Yes," Ruby mumbled. "I keep hearing that." She stared at the fire for a moment, wondering if this was all in vain, if anyone had witnessed the death at all, and if they had, what useful information from it she could mine. After all, from the severe angle on the ground looking up, it was unlikely that anyone would have seen a pusher, if there was one. Likely, they'd have only glimpsed the elf falling. "Any known enemies?" she inquired.

Liberty sighed. "Again, I didn't know him that well. No one did except his inner circle. You should talk to one of them, if you can."

"Do you know their names?"

He nodded slowly, and Ruby wondered for a moment if he'd refuse to provide her this crucial bit of information. "Dalora Greyborn and Magnus Tearwyn are the two I'd point you toward. I'm sure Bron made more friends in the years since he came to town, but those two were the ones he moved here with and the ones I worked with most closely on Tearnanock.

She asked for a description of each, and he supplied it.

"Do owls deliver to Tearnanock?" she asked.

"Oh yeah," he said. "You can be as invisible as you want, but the owls can't be fooled or influenced by any enchantment."

"So I could theoretically send word to one of these elves to speak about what they knew of their dear friend."

"You could, but I would do so with great care. Elves trust Fifth Winds even less than the average person, and they've just lost a long-time friend. You haven't...?"

"No," she said, already knowing where his mind had gone. "If I'd spoken with him, things might be much easier. But it seems that, whatever happened to him, he is at peace with it. Either his death came by his own hand, or he somehow expected whoever did this to give it a shot."

Liberty nodded. "You might tell Magnus and Dalora as much when you speak with them. Knowing their friend is at least at rest in the afterlife will be a great comfort, I'm sure."

Ruby scoffed not impolitely. "I wouldn't go so far as that. But a small comfort, perhaps. And when it comes to death, that's all we can hope for."

Chapter Six

Ruby and Clifford traveled down the footpath through the field, away from Liberty's home and back toward Eastwind. She would send an owl to Magnus Taerwyn and Dalora Greyborn as soon as she could. But for now, the short walk, like the bourbon, was exactly what she needed. She felt a surge of excitement each time the prospect of visiting an invisible avenue crossed her mind. Obviously, it would be visible from the inside... wouldn't it?

She knew it was best not to make any assumptions about magic so far beyond her own abilities, but Liberty's house had been incredibly visible from the inside.

Why did he ever bother to leave it? If he could conjure whatever he needed, he could fill rooms with gold coins.

He could be even richer than Count Sebastian Malavic.

The thought made her feel giddy. Did Malavic realize that? If he didn't, she wanted to be the one to break the news and wipe that perpetually smug expression off the vampire's face. He thought he owned the town with the wealth he'd amassed over the centuries (or millennia—she wasn't sure), but if Liberty had more and could outbid him if need be, then maybe the town wasn't totally doomed by the High Council.

Of course, from what she knew of Liberty's politics, he wasn't nearly as likely to pour money into the town's coffer as Malavic was. It wasn't that Count Malavic was any sort of genuine philanthropist—anyone who'd spent the kind of time around him that she'd been forced to endure would know that. He simply knew that every gold coin he gave to someone was a debt they owed him, even if not explicitly established in the exchange.

Liberty clearly understood that as well, which was exactly why the freed genie was so averse to giving people things that left them feeling indebted.

The town could use a genuinely benevolent philanthropist, though. That way the Sheriff's Department could have the funds to hire a real investigator and Ruby wouldn't be on the hook for this sort of thing. There wasn't even a ghost involved! It seemed like she was getting sucked into cases that didn't play to her strengths more and more, and perhaps that was why she was feeling more jaded than usual about assisting.

Helping solve murders was definitely the right thing to do. Well, *possible* murders. Bron Danann could have simply been depressed or upside down in debts and walked off the edge on his own.

But the berry stains... those *were* suspicious. *5th*. Yes, that didn't look great for her, but there were plenty of other fifths. Maybe he'd lost his mind, thought he was one-*fifth* bat and four-fifths elf and decided to try out his ability to fly. Who knew, really?

Dragon blast! If only she could say "Who knows?" and simply move on. But that wasn't how it worked for her. Nope.

Instead, she had to go from house to house, interviewing people who had very little chance of providing her anything useful.

She stopped by the Pixie Mixie Apothecary on her way, and Kayleigh Lytefoot was generous enough to let her use the store's owl to send messages to the two elves Liberty knew to be closest to the deceased. She wondered if she'd hear back at all.

The next person on her schedule of interviews was Ted. His house, however, was nestled deep in the Deadwoods, and she had no desire to brave the many hidden and not-so-hidden dangers living among those ancient trees. While the werewolves and the occasional werebear or were-elk might enjoy a romp out there, it was less conducive to survival if one was a witch. Clifford would have been fine, but she could hardly expect him to protect both himself and her from his fellow hellhounds or the hidebehinds who were supposedly so good at hiding behind trees that no one ever saw them until they were already being dragged away to be eaten by one.

Ruby had been in the Deadwoods only once, and it was the very same night she'd arrived in Eastwind. It was among that heavy canopy of trees that she'd found herself, post-death and groggy. It was definitely for the best that she hadn't realized what kind of danger she was in at the time, although seeing a giant red dog—she hadn't yet learned about hellhounds—blocking her exit from the dense forest had given her enough of a scare. And then he'd spoken to her telepathically, warning her to be careful in these parts, and offering to chaperone her safely to her next location.

And the rest of her life with Clifford was history.

No, she wasn't going to brave a visit to Ted's shack. But where they had arranged to meet wasn't much safer, if she were being honest.

The Outskirts was a part of Eastwind that most avoided if at all possible. It bordered the Deadwoods on the south end of town and was inhabited almost entirely by werewolves, and not the ones that descended from those who had faired reasonably well following the last great war and now lived in the gated community of Hightower Gardens. The werewolves of the Outskirts were the generational remnants of all the ways the war had beaten and demeaned werekind. And now they'd had three hundred years of eating the bitter fruits planted when the witches came to Eastwind and claimed it as their own. Three hundred years of justified rage that had warped into a culture of meanness and animosity.

And Ruby was walking right into that culture to have a drink with Death.

Chapter Seven

Ted had written that he knew a little place that wasn't half bad where they could grab a drink and chat without all the bustle and conspicuousness of meeting at Sheehan's.

Ruby should have known better than to trust a grim reaper to take safety into account when choosing a location.

As the rows of buildings began to lose stories and spread out, Clifford walked closer by her side, and she could feel his senses heighten. Only once the sparse buildings turned to dilapidated structures where she could almost feel the rot coating her skin if she passed too close by was Ruby sure she'd reached the Outskirts. While it was still currently light outside, she would have to keep her visit with Ted short so she didn't end up here once the sun began to set.

She knew the moment she laid eyes on the shack, even before she saw the sign, that this was the place Ted had designated for their meeting. For one, it was the only building that looked mildly habitable in this area, but it also fit his description: a narrow wooden structure facing the edge of the Deadwoods.

So this was the neighborhood bar, was it?

She walked down the desolate road that ran past it and paused when she saw the sign glowing above the entrance. Pale Horse Saloon.

Were she and Clifford really going to have to enter alone? What if Ted was running late?

But she needn't have worried, because just as she took a step toward the entrance, the reaper's voice called to her. She turned and saw Ted strolling from the direction of the Deadwoods, using his scythe as a hiker might a walking stick. Seemed a bit cavalier to her.

"Right on time," Ruby said, feeling a wave of relief wash through her. But it was short-lived. Because as soon as Ted was only a few yards away, she felt the usual shroud of mortality wrap around her. The reaper carried this grim aura with him everywhere he went. It was just part of the gig. Not that she was especially bothered by the reminder that her life was finite, just that it was hard for that knowledge to coexist with a sense of safety.

"Thankfully, I'm off work today," he said.

"Yes, I'm sure the entire town would be relieved to hear that."

"Heh. You're right. Come on. Let's grab a drink and chat. They always save a booth for me in the corner."

Pale Horse Saloon was about what Ruby had thought it would be, which didn't say much for it. She usually expected the worst in hope that it wouldn't come to pass and she'd be pleasantly surprised—the pessimist's bliss. But in cases like this, when her expectation for the worst was fulfilled, she felt only mild satisfaction in being right.

The place was a dump, to start. Many of the floorboards were rotted out in places, and she had to be careful where she stepped to avoid finding herself trapped up to her knee.

The clientele didn't subvert any of her unkind assumptions, either. They looked ready to round on her, circle her as predators like them would, and then... she shuddered to think of it. The only reason they didn't do that, as far as she could tell, was that she was accompanied by one ferocious hellhound and a grim reaper. Not bad as far as a posse went. She wasn't convinced they respected Ted so much as feared him, but either way, when he looked around, spotted the bartender and said, "They're with me," she could feel some of the roiling aggression in the room subside. Not that it wasn't still there, but it wasn't bolstered by the hope that anything could be done to act upon it.

The bartender only had one eye. But unlike the handful of genuine cyclopses around town, he didn't appear to have been born that way. He wore a leather eye patch, and a thick, raised scar peaked out on either side of it, easily visible even in the dim light.

The corner booth was unoccupied like Ted had said it would be. Ruby settled in carefully on the wooden bench, keeping an eye on a sharp bit of the seat where the wood had cracked and an ornery splinter jutted out, no doubt eager to lodge itself deep into the buttock of the first person feeling spunky enough to slide across it.

Ted brought over two tankards of beer, neither of

which Ruby trusted to be free of grime, the bartender's spit, or even poison. She thanked him for it all the same.

In another situation, Clifford might have made himself comfortable under the table. But under the table seemed to be the only place filthier than the tabletop in this place, and anyway, his hackles remained up and would likely stay that way until they were clear of the Outskirts. So he stood beside her, his back to the wall, front facing every miscreant who might get it in his head to try something.

Ted had no problem putting his back to the rest of the place, and why would he?

"Try it," he said, nodding at her tankard. "It's a great blend. Not too hoppy. They only serve it in the Outskirts."

Try it? She wouldn't even touch her lips to the rim. "Maybe in a moment. I've just come from Liberty Freeman's, and he offered me a drink while I was there."

"Ah, of course he did. Heh. Does that mean you need a little food to sop up the alcohol? They have a delicious stew that they make to help sober up the clientele and keep them drinking. I could order you some."

An image of a large simmering cauldron popped into her mind. The bartender's missing eyeball bubbled to the surface of the broth.

Ruby's stomach clenched. "I'm fine. Thank you, though. Maybe we should get right into it, huh?"

Ted took a long draught from his drink, the lip of the cup disappearing underneath his dark hood for a moment. "Sounds great."

"Perfect. Yesterday, you said you were at the Emporium on business, correct?"

"Yes."

"The business had to do with Bron Dannan's demise."

"It did. Obviously I didn't know who it would be prior to it happening. That's just the way it works with us reapers. Lore has it we used to know, but too many of us kept stepping in and preventing the deaths of our friends. The nepotism didn't go over well with the powers that be, so now we don't know."

"But you know *someone* is about to die, yes?"

"We know someone is in mortal danger and has a very good chance of dying. Every so often, fate or luck intervenes and the death doesn't come to pass. And then we get to go home early. Heh."

"I'm sure you're not the only ones thrilled with that outcome." She raised her arm to grab her drink, then remembered and balled her fingers into a fist that she set firmly in her lap. "So you knew someone was going to die. I assume you were looking for it?"

"I was, but I tell you, that play was something else. So much drama! All the things you would want in a theatrical production—war, star-crossed lovers, betrayal, revenge!"

"You didn't see Bron fall then?"

Ted hung his head. "No, I didn't."

"But you knew the moment he landed, presumably."

He brought his gloved hand up to rub at the back of his neck. "Erm, no, not really."

"You don't get some sort of bodily indication when the death has actually come to pass?"

"I do. But, well, I was so engrossed in the play that when I felt what I usually feel, I assumed it was because Queen Naifa had just died in the arms of her guards."

Ruby tried not to lose patience. "You felt a man die in the way that your kind have been conditioned, if not bred, to feel since the dawn of time, and you thought it was due to a *dramatic performance?*"

"Heh. Well, when you put it like that, it sounds kind of silly. But yeah, that's what happened."

"So it was a while, then, before you put two and two together and discovered the body."

"Probably a few minutes at least, although, the play was so good that I'm not sure how much time passed. It could have been two minutes or two hours." He chuckled and shook his head at what Ruby assumed to be his fond memories of the show.

"According to my mental math, it couldn't have been more than about fifteen minutes." She paused. "Was the play truly that good?"

Ted leaned forward and in a hoarse whisper said, "It was fantastic."

"*Yikes,*" said Clifford. "*No play is that good.*"

"*It is somewhat suspicious, isn't it?*" Ruby replied silently.

"One more question, and then I'll thank you again for the drink and be on my way. After the elf perished, did you complete the job?"

"You mean, did I usher him into the afterlife?"

She nodded.

"Sure did. Right away. He was a little disappointed, but he was ready to go."

"Did he say anything about his death?"

Ted gasped, a hand flying to where his heart might

have been had he possessed one. He leaned away from her like she'd just blasphemed. "No! Absolutely not! Reaper code of ethics requires us not to talk about the death with the dead. Our objective is to get them from one plane to the next without triggering any memories that might cause them to decide not to go. That means no talking about how they died, and no trying to console them with how good of a life they lived."

"Then what do you talk about?"

Ted shrugged a shoulder, and it crackled like eggshells underfoot. "This and that. They usually have questions about where they're going, and I answer them as best as I can, putting a positive spin on it, as the case may be. But mostly we talk about scufflepuck."

"Scufflepuck?" She was familiar with the pastime (one could catch a heated match of it at Sheehan's Pub seven nights a week), but she'd never found it particularly interesting.

He shrugged again. "Yeah, people like talking about it. It calms them."

She decided to drop that topic and get back to the important one. "You're telling me Bron Dannan moved on?"

"I am."

That was huge. She'd suspected as much this far after his death, but the confirmation was critical. She would need to think on it more. But she'd prefer to do it somewhere else.

"That feeling you get when someone is about to be killed," she said. "Do you have it right now?"

Ted cocked his head to the side, silent for a moment, then replied, "Nope."

"Great." She carefully scooted off the bench and stood. "Then I think now's a good time for me to head home." She thanked Ted for the drink she didn't touch, and hurried clear of the Outskirts as quickly as possible, banking on Ted's instincts that she would make it back to the town proper alive.

Chapter Eight

Ruby was already exhausted from walking all over town, but a quick cup of tea at A New Leaf perked her right up. She guessed Clifford was also ready for a long nap, having missed his usual mid-morning, noontime, and early afternoon ones, but he didn't show it as they left the teashop and went to a more upscale locale to meet with the only of the two elves who had agreed to meet on such short notice.

She hadn't received any response from Magnus Taerwyn, but Dalora Greyborn was generous enough to carve out some time for it, though the woman wouldn't degrade herself by meeting somewhere that lacked the necessary class.

That was how it transpired that Ruby, still clad head to toe in loose-fitting black garments, came to arrive at the doorstep of Garden Variety. While she and Clifford waited for the restaurant's host to greet them, she browsed one of the menus tucked into a slot on the host stand. She'd never eaten there or even set foot inside, despite the restaurant having opened its doors long before she'd landed in Eastwind.

She examined the menu and arched an eyebrow at the prices. What she would normally pay at Treetop Lodge for a complete steak dinner could only get her so much as a cup of summer squash soup. And the prices soared even higher when she moved to the list of entrees. There was no trace of meat to be found on the menu. She held it low for Clifford to see, and he scoffed.

"Why even open a restaurant if you're not going to offer meat?"

Ruby shrugged, replaced the menu, and took a quick look around at the early dinner guests. They were mostly elves, but she also spotted a few druids and even a table of four witches. The noise from conversation throughout the dining room was subdued, but of course it was—leafy greens never did rile up a crowd. Everyone was probably feeling a bit foolish for paying so much for something they could easily grow in their own garden.

The hostess, a young witch Ruby didn't recognize from around town greeted her. "Table for one?"

Ruby didn't miss the witch's appraising look. Was she worried she'd be fired for seating a Fifth Wind? She didn't even look at Clifford, which was just fine. It wasn't as if she hadn't seen him there, all fiery fur and hulking bulk. "I'm here to meet Dalora Greyborn. Is she here yet?"

"She just came in. I'll show you to her table."

Dalora's back was to them when they approached, and Ruby admired the elf's sleek copper hair, strands of which hung over the back of her chair, nearly brushing the flagstone floor.

"Mrs. Greyborn?" the hostess said.

When the elf turned to look. Her gaze landed immediately on Ruby, who was momentarily startled into silence by the woman's brilliant emerald eyes. "Mrs. True?" she said.

"Miss, not missus," Ruby corrected her. "And Ruby is just fine."

The hostess left and Ruby settled into the chair opposite. When she looked up again, Dalora's eyes were glued to Clifford as he lowered himself to the ground.

"He comes with me," Ruby said.

"I see that. Is he... your *familiar?*" She said the last word like it stung the tip of her tongue.

Ruby wasn't surprised. For those who weren't witches, familiars were always a strange concept. And because the familiar of every other witch in town was feline, they mostly kept out of sight, sleeping at home while the witches went about their business. Only a few ever brought their cats with them, and why would they in a town where werewolves and werebears were a dime a dozen? Eastwind's weres usually possessed self-control when it came to their hunting instincts, but "usually" by no means meant "always." She had heard more than one rumor over the years about familiars making a narrow escape.

"Yes," Ruby said. "From what I've read, hellhound familiars are as common as Fifth Wind witches. Exactly as common, in fact." She didn't miss Dalora's distasteful flinch at the words "Fifth Wind." The elf's alabaster skin seems impossibly smooth for someone who, by all accounts, was easily over two hundred years old, and even the slightest facial twitch was noticeable on the pristine palette.

"We saw each other just the other day," the elf said.

"Did we?"

"Yes. In Ezra's Magical Outfitters."

Ruby racked her memory. Yes, she had seen an elf leave just as she was entering.

"Are you friends with Ezra Ares?" Dalora asked.

"Yes, you could say that."

The smallest hint of a smile appeared at the corners of Dalora's lips, and she seemed to relax. "He's a good witch."

"He's also a bit of a crook."

At that, the elf finally relaxed as she chuckled. "He doesn't like to play by the rules. At least the ones that don't make sense. I can relate."

"What rules haven't you been playing by lately?" Ruby asked, feigning innocence. There was something about Dalora's demeanor that felt more like armor than simple propriety usually did, and Ruby was determined to get underneath it.

"I wouldn't even know," Dalora replied before sipping the glass of water in front of her. "I don't pay much attention to what is and isn't allowed in Eastwind."

"What about in Tearnanock?"

The elf paused, her almond eyes narrowing. "You know about it?"

"I do. I know a great many things. Part of being a Fifth Wind."

"Bloom told you about it. It had nothing to do with being a Fifth Wind," said Clifford from beside her.

"She doesn't need to know that."

A fairy fluttered over to their table and took their order. It wasn't lost on Ruby that an establishment clearly built to appease the elven population didn't have a single elf working in it. She would be shocked to see an elf "demean" him or herself enough to work in the service industry.

Ruby declined any food, ordering only a hot chamomile tea, but Dalora ordered herself a beet salad with sprinkled goat cheese and diced almonds.

"You know why I asked to meet, don't you?" Ruby asked once the waiter flew away.

"You mentioned Bron in your letter." She paused. "Have you spoken with him?" Her postured stiffened again as she asked it, and her face spoke of having spelled something rotten.

To be fair, there were days when Ruby found speaking with the dead just as unappealing as Dalora seemed to find it.

"No, I haven't spoken with him. I did, however, just speak with Ted a few hours ago and he confirmed that Bron has passed into the beyond without a fight. He's at peace now."

"You don't know that," Clifford corrected.

"What ultimate outcome he earned in his lifetime is a mystery to me. Might as well give her hope he's not being sliced into a thousand pieces."

She didn't have a clear understanding of what happened to spirits once they died, assuming they weren't lingering and dropping in on her all hours of the night. She'd read about reincarnation, and that seemed likely enough. But records of those few who remembered their past lives indicated that quite a bit of time passed between one death and the next birth, and no account was provided for what each soul endured during that in-between time. Was it like the Heaven and Hell of the Bible? She doubted it, partially because she knew both Heaven and Hell to merely be two realms among the many, not supernatural spaces reserved for the souls of the dead.

Dalora's expression showed only the tiniest hint of emotion at the mention of her friend moving on, but what that emotion was, was indecipherable to Ruby.

"Do you have any reason to believe Bron would have jumped from the clock tower of his own accord?"

The elf wasted no time shaking her head. "No. He would never. He was too proud to do that, and he had no reason to."

"Was he depressed? In debt?"

"Absolutely not. Bron and I have been friends for centuries. We can share anything with each other. He's had hard times like that before and told me about them. I have no reason to believe he would suddenly start keeping such things from me. We've always had each other's back. Or rather, we did. And now..." It was the closest she'd come to genuine sadness—a mere flicker of her slim nostrils.

"What do you think happened to him, then?"

She shrugged. "Murder is the only thing I can think of."

"What did he do for a living?"

"Nothing. He had money." She paused. "Sometimes he fixed clocks for a hobby."

Elves were renowned for their skills in horology, and most of the clocks in Eastwind were elven. They kept time flawlessly without an ounce of magic. It made sense that Bron would do that as a way to both pass time and remind everyone of his lineage.

And the fact that an elf had fallen from the very tallest clock in Eastwind had not been lost on Ruby. But not even her Insight had a clue as to how that might be significant. "Could he have been servicing the clock?" she asked. "Perhaps he fell and it was a simple accident."

But Dalora scoffed. "You aren't familiar with the history of the clock tower, are you?"

Ruby cocked her head to the side. "I suppose not. Care to enlighten me?"

The waiter set down Ruby's tea and Dalora's salad. The beets *did* look delicious. Not delicious enough to warrant the cost, though.

The elf tucked in before going on. "It's official name is Fallia's Eye, though no one has called it that in years. No, now it's just 'the clock tower.'" Her tone made it clear that she was not keen on this development. "It was a gift from King Precion, a token of peace when the first elves discovered Eastwind."

"Not sure how they discovered a realm that already had people living in it," Clifford muttered.

"It was an elf-made masterpiece for generations. And then through misuse and poor handling, it eventually needed maintenance—elven clocks don't require that if properly cared for—and rather than bringing in an elven clockmaker from Fallia, they used *magic.*" She stabbed at her salad like the beets had insulted her. "Once you use magic on a masterpiece like that, it's never the same. No elf will touch it."

"Which means Bron wasn't up there to maintain it," Ruby concluded for her.

"Exactly. He wouldn't have been caught dead." She cleared her throat and straightened her spine. "Poor choice of words."

Ruby allowed her a moment to work on the salad and regroup while she served herself some tea. The calming chamomile scent wafted up to meet her nostrils as soon as she peeked under the lid. She held it open a bit longer than necessary, hoping to give Dalora a dose of it as well. Goddess knew the uptight elf could use it.

Finally, Ruby said, "Do you know of anyone who would have wanted to push Bron from the clo— from Fallia's Eye?"

The use of its official name had the intended effect, and Dalora didn't hesitate to respond. "Ignatius Hopper."

Ruby couldn't disguise her shock at hearing that name. Hopper was a well respected figure in Eastwind society. He'd been pleasant to Ruby and Clifford on the two occasions they'd crossed paths. Werebunnies didn't usually take to Clifford, but Hopper had gone so far as to toss the hellhound the last half of a ham sandwich once simply because her familiar was slobbering conspicuously at the scent of it. "And why do you believe Ignatius Hopper might have pushed Bron from the tower?"

"Ignatius had asked that Bron work on an elven clock he had. Bron agreed. They used to be friends, you know. They got along quite well. But when Bron told Ignatius he would need more time to work on the piece, Ignatius grew impatient. Well, you know how long a truly unique timepiece can take to fix once an unskilled hand has tinkered with it"—Ruby did not, but decided not to mention it—"but Ignatius wanted it fixed right away. Bron reminded him that he wasn't getting paid for the work and that he would take as long as he needed to return it to its original quality. It went on like that for a while. And recently, it escalated."

"Escalated to the point of murder, you think?"

Dalora shrugged. "Possibly. You know how those werebeasts are. They can just snap."

Ruby hadn't found this to be more true for weres than it was for anyone, but she nodded along.

"When you say it escalated...?"

"Oh, letters and such. Ignatius didn't know how to get into Tearnanock Estates, so hate mail was about as much as he could do so long as Bron stayed within our community. And I urged him to do so until he could fix the clock. But he clearly didn't listen."

"And how long had he been working on this clock prior to his death?"

She considered it. "Perhaps four or five years."

Ruby choked slightly on her tea. "Four or five years?"

"Ah yes. Of course that would seem like a long time to a short-lifer like you. Ignatius felt the same. But all great things take time."

Ruby ignored the slight. "I understand the disagreement, but I also know Hopper to be one of the more decent people in Eastwind. I have a hard time imagining him committing murder over a clock."

"He accused Bron of stealing it. He said he'd find out where Bron lived and take it back himself if he had to, but he was going to get it back one way or another."

Ruby still wasn't convinced, but for the sake of

propriety, she nodded. "I understand. I'll pass the tip along to the sheriff and have her look into it."

That seemed to pacify the elf enough that she returned to her salad.

"Just to cover all the angles," Ruby said a moment later, "you can't think of anyone else in town who would have wanted him dead?"

Dalora's eyes locked onto Ruby's, as if trying to read between the lines. At last, she said, "No. I can't think of a single other person in Eastwind who might go to those lengths."

There it was, then. No help whatsoever.

It was unusual for Ruby to wish a ghost would visit her, but in a strange case like this, she found herself longing for just that. Surely, Bron would have had more useful information.

"One last question," Ruby said, "and then I'll leave you to your delicious salad."

Dalora Greyborn pressed her rosy lips into a thin line and arched her eyebrows expectantly.

"Do the words, 'the fifth' have any meaning at all to you?"

Dalora blinked and a shadow seemed to cross her face. Then she set her jaw and smoothed her expression until it reminded Ruby of the surface of quiet pond on a windless day. "You mean other than the Fifth Wind I'm speaking to right now?"

"Yes, other than that."

"No. It has no meaning. And at the same time, it could have a thousand meanings."

"I understand. Nothing specific, then?"

"No. Nothing comes to mind."

It didn't take Sheriff Bloom's angelic abilities of judgment to know Dalora was hiding something. But it also didn't take a genius to know Ruby wouldn't be squeezing an ounce of that information from the elf, no matter how hard she tried.

"Very well," Ruby said. "Thank you for your time. I'll keep you apprised if we discover anything else about Ignatius Hopper."

Which meant, of course, that they would likely never speak again. And that was just fine with Ruby.

She and Clifford left the restaurant and waited until she was home before sending an owl to Bloom. It was well past dinnertime, and Ruby was ready to call it a day.

However, there was still work to be done.

She wrote, "*Spoke with Dalora Greyborn. Does Ignatius Hopper have an alibi for time of death?*"

And then she sent the message on its way and plucked a few of her favorite vegetables from the garden boxes behind her house. A beet salad didn't sound half bad. Especially when it didn't cost her a thing.

Chapter Nine

Sheriff Bloom was grateful for the beautiful morning. As she strolled beneath the nurturing May sunshine, she carried a giant chocolate croissant with her. She'd been saving it for whenever she could get away from her desk and truly savor it. But a few minutes prior, she'd reached the point when all she could think about was the croissant sitting uneaten in its box. And so her progress on the stacks and stacks of paperwork around her office—some forms she had to fill out, others she had to review and sign, and others still that simply needed a moment of her time to be filed away—had come to a grinding halt.

Nothing to do about it except take her break a few minutes early.

She bit into the pastry as she descended the stairs away from the sheriff's department and was forced to plant her feet firmly under her, at risk of falling over from the decadence. The taste was all encompassing, and it wouldn't do to trip and fall down the stairs. Not only would it likely be painful, but if someone saw it, well, that was just plain undignified and below the station she held.

But most importantly, it might damage the rest of the croissant.

After the initial wave of euphoria began to subside, she carefully scaled the stairs and made her way to Fulcrum Park where she was scheduled to meet Ruby True and recap the events of the previous day.

She hadn't been able to do nearly as much investigative work on her own as she'd hoped, but she'd done about as much as she'd expected, which was virtually nothing outside of having Deputy Titterfield check on Ignatius Hopper's alibi for Bron Danann's time of death. Fortunately, a life in the bureaucratic realm of Heaven had prepared her well for her cloistered life within the confines of her office.

But Heaven didn't have chocolate croissants. It didn't have any food at all.

She paused momentarily in her progress, wondering if she hadn't been in Hell the whole time after all.

But no. Way too many harps for it to have been Hell. She'd heard *that* realm preferred accordions.

Either way, she much preferred life in Eastwind. And it was while she was in the midst of her gratitude for her present place and time that she spotted Ruby walking down one of the spoke-like streets leading to the inner ring of town, the center of which was marked with the lively Fulcrum Fountain.

It was a perfect day to enjoy a walk-and-talk, and Bloom suspected that even though she didn't have many pertinent updates, that didn't mean they would have nothing to discuss regarding the case.

Ruby True was sporting her usual black attire from head to toe, and with her wild, fiery hair, at a distance she resembled a lit black candle. But up close, like she was now, she looked like the last person one would want to tell she looked like a lit black candle.

Only a fool would have observed at the small stature of Ruby and mistaken her for anything other than a formidable opponent in whatever the situation may arise. She had that look about her, a keenness in her eyes that Bloom had noted the first time she'd come to check in on Eastwind's new Fifth Wind so many years before. And the fact that the witch kept that mammoth familiar with her wherever she went also tamped down the urge to do or say anything that would set her off.

"Did you bring enough for me?" Ruby asked, Clifford following just a step behind her.

"Nope. I didn't even bring enough for me." The sheriff popped the last bite into her mouth and licked her fingertips shamelessly. The real shame would have been in *not* licking them.

"Then how about," Ruby proposed, "we stroll on down to the bakery to appease both of our cravings, and I'll fill you in on my busy day yesterday."

"Sounds like a plan." They started down one of the long spokes toward the bakery.

"You know," Ruby said, "it's really not fair that you can eat as much as you want and never gain weight."

"Who said I can't gain weight?"

Ruby's eyebrows raised in interest. "I guess I just assumed your metabolism was also unchanging. Plus, I've never seen an overweight angel."

Bloom grinned. "Flying really burns the calories."

Ruby chuckled. "Did you get my message about Ignatius Hopper?"

"I did. Titterfield looked into it."

"And?"

"Hopper was in Avalon on the day Bron fell."

Ruby arched a brow. "You're sure?"

"He was there with a whole fuffle of werebunnies on their way to the Grand Vegetable Gardens of Golth. They backed up his story."

Ruby grunted. "Figures. I couldn't see someone like him pushing another living being to their death."

"Me neither. It sounds like you got up to some trouble yesterday, though. Care to fill me in?"

Ruby provided quite a rundown of events, so that by the time they reached the bakery at the outer edge of the Emporium, Bloom's racing thoughts alone might have burned off the calories of another half dozen chocolate croissants.

They ordered their pastries—only one each, plus a sausage wrap for Clifford—and stepped out of the delectable smelling bakery and into the Emporium. While many vendors had already set up their carts for the day, the place was mostly devoid of any shoppers. But it was early on a Thursday, so that was to be expected; those with plans to grab a bite to go or check off their to-do lists on their lunch hour hadn't yet managed to make a break from their jobs.

Bloom checked the time on the large clock tower. It was only five past eleven. But her eyes remained glued to the clock face as a thought, previously buried under the rubble of her mundane daily tasks, surfaced for air. "What time did you say the play began?"

"Hmm?" The croissant hung half out of Ruby's mouth as she turned her head then followed Bloom's eyes up to the clock. She bit off the piece and chewed it hurriedly until she was able to speak around it, though her words were still rather muffled. "E-eh-en i-dy."

Bloom let her gaze fall back to the quiet Emporium. "Seems like a strange time to start a play. Why not wait until noon?"

Ruby swallowed audibly. "Are you asking me to explain the behavior of actors?"

She wouldn't dare. "It just seems strange, doesn't it? An elf falls from a tower and no one sees it because everyone is watching a play that begins at an unusual time."

"That seems to be the line I've heard from everyone I've spoken to so far," Ruby said. "But I follow where you're leading. You think the play might have been an intentional distraction."

"A successful one at that."

Ruby pulled off another flakey piece of pastry and popped it in her mouth. "Then I suppose speaking with the actors might be necessary."

"First," Bloom said, "we have to figure out who they are."

"Oh! I know where to find that!"

Bloom jerked her head around. "You do?"

Ruby nodded. "But you're going to want to hurry and finish that on the short walk over. You know the Lytefoots don't allow any outside food."

Bloom let out an "Ahh..." and nodded. "Of course. The bulletin board."

It was a shame to rush through something as

enjoyable as her chocolate treat, but that was how her life went as sheriff. Sometimes the best parts of her day had to be rushed, and the worst parts dragged on forever...

Chapter Ten

Before Ruby could enter the front door of the Pixie Mixie Apothecary, she felt Bloom's hand on her shoulder to stop her. She turned, wondering what dire warning the sheriff was just about to deliver. The angel loved dire warnings. She had a flare for the dramatic, that one.

Bloom stared her dead in the eyes, an air of urgency emanating from her large pupils. "Do I have any chocolate on my face?"

Ah. Not a dire warning then. "Just a little, there." Ruby pointed to a spot above her own lip, and the sheriff wiped the corresponding bit of skin on her face. "No, no," Ruby said. "A little higher. Just there."

"Did I get it?" Bloom murmured, her eyes darting around to make sure no one else was witnessing the interaction.

"Yes, all better."

Bloom rolled her shoulders back, her giant white wings extending slightly before folding again against her back. "Great." She nodded for Ruby to go ahead and proceed inside.

"*Not nice,*" Clifford chided.

"*What?*" Ruby responded defensively.

"*There was nothing on her face.*"

"*I know that. But far be it from me to forfeit an opportunity to provide an angel with a little humility.*"

"*Good point.*"

The bell above the door of the Pixie Mixie jingled as they entered, and Ruby's Insight bristled. But before she could take a crack at why that might be, they were spotted by Kayleigh Lytefoot.

The pixie was busy helping a customer in the fungal aisle, but she waved and said she'd be with them in a second. The customer, an ogre who Ruby had seen around town, generally in the seedier parts, clearly noted who had just walked in, and his eyes went wide.

Ah yes. It was so nice to know that *she* wasn't the cause of alarm this time. No, an ogre wouldn't have any issue with a Fifth Wind. But a small-time criminal like the one next to Kayleigh would definitely be wary of the sheriff.

They approached the bulletin board off to the side of the entrance, and Ruby gazed over the various flyers, looking for the proper playbill.

Her eyes jumped from an announcement of free tutoring to Mancer Academy students struggling in aeromancy, to another that announced the grand opening of Eastwind's first ever all-inclusive spa (Ruby wasn't sure if that meant it included everything one could want in a spa for a single price, or it didn't turn away customers based on upon creature type). After a handwritten bulletin that simply said, *"Meet me behind the entrance to the Parchment Catacombs at midnight. You know who you are!"* held her attention for a long moment, Bloom said, "Here we go!" and pointed to a black-and-white sheet of parchment with a wooden thumbtack holding it to the board.

While none of the individual performers were listed, they did discover that the troop was called The Rambling Mummers. Quite a peculiar name, but when Ruby remarked that *any* group of performers could claim "rambling" in their title and not be wrong, Bloom shot her a look that told her the judgment wasn't welcome.

The avenging angel had a lot of nerve implying *that*. But perhaps she had a point; judging any person of interest based upon something as trivial as a troop name wasn't helpful in an investigation.

"It says there's another performance today. Same time," Bloom said, pointing to the information. "Tuesday, Thursday, and Saturday. This week only." She grinned. "What do you say, catch a show with me in a few?"

Ruby groaned. "I suppose it could be helpful. At least we can speak with the troop leader afterward."

Ruby glanced down at the flyer again. If she knew anything about the way actors' egos functioned, the leader of the Rambling Mummers would also be the star of the production, and *that* was likely the woman whose sketched image adorned the very center of the playbill. Her round fairy face was almost childlike, but that was par for the course with her kind. While the image was in black and white, the plumpness of the fairy's lips led Ruby to believe she would regularly wear a shocking crimson lipstick to draw even more attention to her main facial feature. Meanwhile, the fairy's eyes were nothing to write home about, just little beady things, each disappearing under a thick curtain of undoubtedly fake eyelash.

No, if they succeeded in pinning down this woman for a word, it wouldn't be the highlight of Ruby's day. And not just because it had stiff competition against the chocolate croissant.

The ogre finished his transaction with Kayleigh and scurried out of the store, avoiding eye contact with both Ruby and Bloom as he went. He ambled with a slight hunch, like he was trying to conceal what he'd just bought, but it was tricky to be sure, since ogres were always a little hunched by nature.

"A word, Kayleigh?" asked the sheriff.

The pixie fluttered over, and they met her halfway. Her wings beat rapidly, but the rest of her demeanor spoke of a calm confidence. Kayleigh, with her waist-length flowing golden hair and regally sloped nose, was outstandingly beautiful, and if the woman had not also had wings and been all of three feet tall, Ruby might have felt a slight tinge of jealousy. But as it was, they weren't competing for any of the same men. In fact, not only was it *never* actually a competition between women like the menfolk often wanted them to believe, but she and Kayleigh weren't even both competing for men. Kayleigh had long ago settled down with her partner, Stella, and the two of them showed no romantic interest in anyone else, male, female, or otherwise.

Years ago, while Ruby was still in the tumult of her doomed relationship with Ezra Ares, she'd asked Kayleigh how she'd known Stella was the one she wanted to spend her life with. The conversation took an unexpected turn when Kayleigh explained that it wasn't so much that she was never interested in men, just that if she was committing the rest of her life to a single person, she couldn't see the sense in making it a man. Pixies were long-lifers, and she'd rather spend hundreds of years with a woman. Also, she'd gone on to say, she did love Stella like no one she'd ever met. And once Ruby had gotten to know the reclusive and science-minded Stella better, she could understand why.

Ruby had never told Kayleigh, or anyone for that matter, how much that conversation had changed the course of her life. Because at the time, she'd actually been considering the option Ezra had presented her of stopping the aging process along with him, so the two of them could *not* grow old together. Did she want to not grow old together with a man?

The prospect did seem a bit tedious. She had very few friends and had always felt more herself in the company of other women—Clifford excluded.

The heart-to-heart with Kayleigh long ago hadn't necessarily made the decision for her on what to do about Ezra, but maybe, just maybe, the compelling argument had been the speck of dust that tipped the scales.

"Is anyone else in the store?" Bloom asked.

Kayleigh shook her head. "Official business, then?"

"Sort of. Do you know anything about the actors involved in this play?" she held out the flyer that she'd pulled from the wall.

The pixie inspected it for a moment, then looked up, a suspicious grin on her face. "Why would I know about this? You think all fae hang out together?"

Bloom's lips pressed into a thin line as Ruby stifled a laugh.

"Of course I don't think that," Bloom chided. "But you see people come in and out of here all day and—"

Kayleigh held up a delicate hand. "I know, I know, Sheriff. I'm just giving you a hard time." She paused and looked at the flyer again before continuing. "They're fairies. Pixies and fairies don't get on well. Not that I have a bias against them, but I would assume they'd have one against me."

Ruby decided to step in. She generally did this whenever a strange cultural nuance was hinted at. Although Bloom had been around for a while, there were still plenty of things regarding the different groups that the angel hadn't learned. Meanwhile, Ruby was a relative newcomer, and it required swallowing much less pride for *her* to inquire further into things like this than it would the sheriff. So she said, "I'm not familiar with this animosity. Why wouldn't fairies like pixies?"

Kayleigh sighed. "It's just a holdover from Fallia, our home realm. We're all fae, so I don't personally see why the details matter, but back home, what type of fae you were made all the difference to how you were treated. The elves run everything, even though they constitute the smallest subset of fae. They're the tallest and the strongest, and so"—she shrugged—"you know how it goes. I believe ogres are technically fae, but they left the realm long ago and never looked back. I don't blame them."

"But the fairies and pixies?"

"Right. The two underclasses. Anytime the elves felt like they might be losing their power, they would launch subtle campaigns to turn the fairies and the pixies against one another. It was all propaganda, but the elves were great at it."

Bloom nodded solemnly. "Can't have an uprising if the underclasses are busy fighting against themselves."

"Precisely," said Kayleigh. "That's all it was. But after millennia of it, people start to actually believe it deep in their fibers. That was just one of the many reasons Stella and I decided to relocate to Eastwind instead."

Ruby said, "It's not always better here."

Kayleigh smiled politely. "It's *always* better here. Even when it's at its worst."

"So you haven't heard anything about the performance?" Bloom prompted again.

"Only that it's engrossing."

Bloom frowned. "Right. We've heard that."

"Over and over again," Ruby added.

After thanking Kayleigh for her time, they made for the Emporium. It seemed that watching the play had become an inevitable part of this investigation, no matter how little desire Ruby had to subject herself to it.

"I had a thought," she said as the first sliver of the Emporium came into view between buildings down the road.

"That's always a good sign," replied Bloom.

"So far, no one we've spoken to who was in the Emporium that day saw Bron Danann fall because they all had their backs to the clock and were facing the stage."

"Mm-hm."

"But the actors were facing the crowd, which means they could have also seen the top of the tower above everyone's head."

Bloom nodded and didn't speak right away, which

Ruby took to mean her theory was sound. Finally, the sheriff said, "All the more reason to speak with the troop."

Of course, if the actors themselves had anything to do with the death, then there was little chance of getting useful information out of them. But as far as she could surmise, their maximum contribution to the situation could be no more than, perhaps, supplying a convenient distraction for whomever had wished to push the elf... if that had been the circumstance.

It was like trying to complete a connect-the-dots picture when you could only see every sixth dot. Was it a horse? A baseball? A lemon meringue pie? But that was what investigation was for, to collect all the data points. And they had only begun to do so.

The first resonant toll from the bell tower at the heart of the Emporium caused Ruby to jump just as they entered the open-air market. Was it noon already?

The place was crowded, and where Ruby and Bloom had entered the Emporium put them just to the left of the stage. Standing shoulder to shoulder, with Clifford sitting just ahead of them, they both observed the movements of the actors. The production was already ten minutes in, judging by the noon bells. The angel allowed Ruby to entertain her theory that the actors themselves could have seen Bron Danann fall, and she gazed up toward Fallia's Eye. Even without the added leverage of a stage, she had a clear view of the edge of the upper lookout.

Most of the bell tower was solid all the way up, all four sides a smooth stone that might have been rough before time itself got the best of it. The top was, by Ruby's estimate, fifty feet high. But toward the top, the smooth sides opened up to better allow the bells to echo through town, and four stone columns, one at each corner, extended for perhaps eight feet to brace the rounded roof. It would have been from the platform between those columns where Bron had jumped. Forty feet straight down to an unforgiving cobblestone landing.

Sure enough, she could see that area just fine from where she stood so near to the stage. Were anyone to stand at the edge of that drop, she could have easily spotted it. She knew about the concept of the fourth wall actors went on about, but surely even that couldn't have obscured their view of the elf as he plummeted. Why had none said a word about it? Was it a case of *the show must go on?* Seemed like it wasn't entirely up to them to decide such a thing when a man had just fallen to his death.

The introduction tune of the bells completed, and the presumably largest in the collection began to ring out the noon hour.

Doooom...

What had the actors seen? Was it *just* Bron Danann up there? Or was there someone else who had pushed him? Had he stood at the precipice for a moment, staring out, examining the distance between him and the ground, or had he hastily appeared out of the shadows and stepped off without a second thought?

Doooom...

She tried to imagine it herself, and for a shadow of a moment, she believed herself to be doing an exceptional job of it. But then she realized it wasn't her *imagination* projecting that tall elvish figure on to the top of the tower, creeping closer to the edge...

Doooom...

Someone *else* was there. Another elf. He or she—it was impossible to tell from this distance when all elves wore their hair long—stood on the edge, looking straight ahead. Ruby's heart raced, and her breath threatened to recoil deep into her lungs.

Doooom...

She'd only just managed to point and shout, "Gabby!" before the elf took a step over the edge and dropped out of view.

Chapter Eleven

Ruby braced herself for the sound of the impact, of bone on stone. But she never heard it. The twelfth and final teeth-rattling toll of the bell must have drowned it out.

And meanwhile, not a single person in the crowd seemed to notice.

What they did notice, however, was Sheriff Gabby Bloom soaring low over their heads at what seemed to be mach speed.

Ruby's brain only vaguely registered the voices of the actors as they continued their play despite the new development and the waning focus of the audience. Consummate professionals, clearly.

Clifford helped clear a path between the sardined bodies, making a beeline for where the elf was undoubtedly lying dead on the cobblestones. She wasn't looking forward to the sight, but she was obligated toward it nonetheless.

When she was finally able to push free from the throngs, she discovered Bloom kneeling, her wings still partially extended as if ready to take off at a moment's notice.

Ruby rushed to her side, bracing herself for whatever gore might await her.

But there was none. Sheriff Bloom was holding the elf in her arms, and Ruby gasped when she saw who it was. Although Dalora Greyborn looked quite out of sorts, she didn't look gravely injured or dead.

Movement at the corner of her eye caused Ruby to tear her attention from the elf to look at Ted, who was looming nearby. The reaper shifted on his feet awkwardly and rubbed absently at his left arm once he was noticed. "I guess I'm not needed here anymore. Heh. Nice catch, Sheriff." Without another word, he turned and left the Emporium.

Unfortunately, a murmur was already starting to spread through the crowd, beginning with those in the back who had only to turn to see the strange scene taking place behind them—an even stranger one, no doubt, than the spectacle that had been taking place in front of them on the stage.

And in her initial confusion, Ruby had missed one crucial detail. But thankfully Clifford had not. She hadn't even seen him leave, and suddenly he was returning, a cloth in his jowls. He offered it up to Bloom who quickly pulled it from him and draped it over the elf, covering up the familiar berry stains on her shirt.

While Ruby was well aware that Bron Danann had written *5th* on his shirt, and the knowledge wasn't precisely pleasant. But seeing it for herself on a second elf's clothing, Dalora's nonetheless, sent chills down her spine, and she was no longer keen on keeping her back to the rest of the crowd.

Bloom stood, the unconscious elf in her arms now wrapped snugly with the cloth.

It was almost a burial shroud, Ruby thought.

The angel turned to her. "Meet me at the healing house." And then she extended her wings, causing those closest in the crowd to take a quick step back, and she launched herself skyward.

* * *

Sheriff Bloom knew it would take Ruby a fair bit of time to make her way from the Emporium to Hemlock Healing House on foot. She could have cut the time in half by simply taking a broom, but the Fifth Wind had sworn those off not long after she'd tried it for the first time years ago and nearly landed herself in the healing house straight away.

She stared down at Dalora Greyborn, who was sleeping peacefully in a soft bed by the window. Hemlock had set her up with a room right away, which was not unexpected. Many institutions in Eastwind worked as fast as a worm crawled, but the healing house wasn't among them. Every person working within these walls showed genuine care and concern for the patients, and Bloom got along with them well because of it.

A shiver ran down her spine when she thought about how close the elf had come to lying in a grave instead. Inches. If Ruby hadn't so inarticulately hollered her name and pointed at the precise moment she had...

Not for the first time, Bloom was relieved to know

Ruby had Clifford by her side. If anyone had managed to glimpse the words on Dalora's shirt before she could cover it, word would travel fast, and rumors weren't known for painting anyone in a favorable light. To have one elf paint such a thing on its clothing just before jumping was a strange enough oddity, but twice was something else entirely.

Someone or some *ones* were trying to send a message. That was obvious enough.

There was a knock on the thick oak door of the private suite, and a moment later, Ruby peeked her head in. Bloom motioned for her to enter.

"They said Cliff had to wait outside," Ruby griped. Her curly hair was in quite a tangle, and barring any massive storm blowing in as the cause, it was clear she'd hurried over as quickly as she could. Her cheeks held a little extra color in them from the exertion.

"Do you want me to talk to them?" Bloom offered. Her line of work meant she knew each of the healers by name. She also knew the names of their spouses and children; that wasn't part of the job, it was just good manners and came in handy when she needed to butter them up.

Ruby waved it off and absentmindedly patted her hair. "No, no. He's happier out there, I think." She took a seat across from Bloom, near the foot of the bed. "What's the latest with her?"

"She'll be fine. I was able to stop her before she hit the ground, thanks to your sharp eye."

"And articulate reaction, too, huh?" Ruby said dolefully.

Bloom chuckled quietly. "You said all that needed to

be said to save her life."

"Oh, please. *You* saved her life. Had it been Deputy Titterfield with me, my inane shout-and-point method wouldn't have done much to cushion her fall." She leaned forward in her chair to look again at the elf in the bed. "Dalora Greyborn. I can't believe it."

"I wouldn't either, if I hadn't seen it all happen with my own eyes."

Ruby said, "Her shirt."

Bloom nodded. "I think I covered it up in time. That was quick thinking by Clifford. I always forget he can read. I'll bring him a treat next time I see him."

"Even still. This was the second time someone has fallen from the clock tower after having painted—"

A stirring next to them cut Ruby's words short, and she jumped to her feet to see what was happening.

Bloom leaned forward, putting her elbow on the side of the bed, and brushed a few strands of blonde hair from Dalora's forehead as the elf mumbled. Would she wake enough to speak? Bloom knew she could make it happen, could rouse the woman simply by laying hands on her and summoning the right intentions, but that wasn't always a huge success. Sometimes the body remained asleep to avoid pain. If Dalora had become injured prior to the fall, perhaps in a tussle with an assailant, waking her prematurely could land her in undue agony.

But she was spared the decision as, slowly, the elf's eyes opened.

She blinked, looked around groggily, and when she spotted the sheriff's face hovering over her, she smiled blissfully. Bloom was aware her appearance did that to many people. She was often described as beautiful, but there was more magic to it than that. She came from Heaven, and for all the unfortunate parts of that place, those who left it still carried the peace of it with them wherever they went. The contagious serenity had helped her calm a frantic suspect or victim more times than she could count. And now it was helping bring Dalora Greyborn calmly back to consciousness. Until...

The elf's eyes shot open, and she gasped and tried to sit up. Bloom gently but firmly held her down.

"What happened?" Dalora asked. "Where am I? Why are you here?"

Bloom shushed her and she began to settle down until she noticed the tiny black-clad woman at the foot of her bed. "Why is *she* here? Oh Mother Earth! Am I dead?"

Ruby cleared her throat, no doubt to cover her snickering.

"No, you're alive and well and not in trouble," Bloom assured her. "Relax, and we'll explain everything. Ruby? Would you mind fetching her a cup of water? And don't tell the healers yet."

Ruby left the room, and Dalora calmed even more. "Does anything hurt?" Bloom asked.

The elf scrunched up her face and moved various parts of her body. "No. Nothing. I have a bit of a headache, though. And I'm hungry."

Bloom nodded. "Both of those can be easily cured."

"What happened? How did I get here?"

"You were nearly injured, but I saved you and brought you here to have the healers check on you. I don't believe there will be any lasting injuries if there are any to begin with."

Ruby slipped back into the room and waited until Bloom had helped the elf into a comfortable sitting position before handing her the cup. She drank it all in one tilt.

When she handed the empty cup back to Ruby, the witch asked, "Were you watching the play?"

Dalora nodded.

"And what is the last part of it that you remember?"

After a moment's pause, she said, "The revolution was in full swing, and the guards had taken the queen up to the highest tower to defend her."

Bloom arched an eyebrow at Ruby. Even though neither of them had truly watched the play yet, it wasn't a bad question to ask. However, it carried heavy implication she didn't like, which was that at some point, Dalora had stopped remembering things. The response to her next question was crucial. "What prompted you to write on your shirt?"

The elf's face scrunched. "Huh?"

"Your shirt had some... never mind. What was your goal in climbing the stairs of the clock tower?"

Her face un-scrunched in a hurry as her eyes went wide in alarm. "I did what?"

For Heaven's sake. She didn't remember any of it. It was as Bloom had feared.

She shared a quick glance with Ruby, who nodded.

It looked like she needed a psychic on the case after all. Because a black-out like what Dalora seemed to have experienced could only mean a few things, and one frightening possibility now rose to the top of Bloom's list: possession.

Chapter Twelve

"Remind me who else Liberty suggested you speak with when you interviewed him?" It had already been a long day, and it wasn't even four in the afternoon. The hot sun felt amazing on Bloom's skin, though, after the chilly air of the healing house.

Ruby walked between the sheriff and Clifford. After a quick stop by a sandwich stand, the hellhound appeared in a bit of a coma from devouring the slab of roast beef Bloom had bought him as a reward for his quick thinking, but despite that he was doing an outstanding job of presenting as a protective and intimidating guard.

"He mentioned Dalora Greyborn and... shoot. What was the other one's name?" Ruby struggled with it, running through a few sounds aloud before giving in and saying, "Clifford, do you remember it?" A pause, then, "Ah, yes. You're right. Nothing gets through that steel trap." She patted him on the head. "Magnus Taerwyn. I suppose we should go check in with him soon, shouldn't we?"

"Probably so," replied Bloom as they passed through Fulcrum Park and headed toward the south side of town. "But where we're going now seems like a higher priority at the moment, don't you think?"

"My Insight says yes. I feel like Magnus is likely safe for the moment. However my body is screaming for tea."

"It'll have to wait. But I suspect you'll be offered tea when we meet with them."

"And should I drink it?" Ruby mused.

"I'll leave that to Clifford's judgment."

The hound had a nose that was beyond skilled, as far as Bloom was concerned. It was magical. His scent training had definitely helped him identify different poisonous elements in foods, drinks, and so on, but there was really no accounting for the few times he'd sniffed out a magical spell that had saved Ruby's hide.

Because they'd missed the end of the play and not had a chance to speak with the actors afterward, they'd been forced to do some old-school questioning around the Emporium after they left the healing house. Finally, a minotaur had stoically divulged that he had seen them checking in at the Ram's Head Inn. Bloom hadn't read into the stoicism too much, since minotaurs were always that way.

So that's where they were heading now.

"You asked her what was the last thing she remembered," Bloom said finally, though she still wasn't able to picture a complete theory surrounding her new suspicion.

"Yes," Ruby said, "I did ask that. And she seems to have lost time."

"You thinking what I'm thinking?"

"I assume so, but I just don't see how it could play in." Ruby chewed her bottom lip for a moment as they walked. "An angry spirit? A necromancer flying below the radar? Some other magic entirely? There are potions that can lead to a loss of memory and high suggestibility."

"Right. And then there's the possibility that the trauma from the fall stole away those last moments leading up to it. A good bit of fear can do that."

"Any visible head trauma?"

"None. I checked. I only just caught her in time, and her head snapped back a little. I was worried it might have hit the ground. But there was no swelling, and at that speed, there would have been. She'll have a stiff neck, but I don't think a concussion could be to blame for the memory lapse."

"Then I suppose we need to gather more information."

"I suppose you're right."

There was no lack of small hotels and bed and breakfasts around Eastwind, places where wealthy weekenders from Avalon could stay to relax and enjoy the slower (and cheaper) way of life in this realm. But that would undoubtedly all change once Cair Crestfall opened up in the high-end shopping district. Avalonians only *thought* they wanted a genuine Eastwind experience. But as soon as luxury accommodations were available, they would no doubt choose those instead, only venturing out into the rest of the town in short spurts to feel like they got an authentic experience without gaining too much exposure to the locals. And then the tiny hotels and bed and breakfasts would have to close down.

It was unfortunate. And yet, if the Ram's Head Inn shuttered its doors forever, Bloom wouldn't be too upset. The old stone building was located on the edge of the Outskirts, and that location made perfect sense for the seedier dealings that went on in the stagnant old rooms. But it was, ahem, *affordably* priced, and she supposed that if an entire troop wanted to stay together, that was likely the best place for it. Perhaps the hotel's reputation for turning a blind eye to illicit activity had nothing to do in the fairies' pick of location.

The wooden sign for it hung at an odd angle in front of the door, one of the two metal hinges having apparently rusted out.

"Can't say the guests aren't warned," Ruby remarked.

Bloom entered into the lobby first, instinctually clearing the way of any danger before she let Ruby in behind her.

A long bench made from a cross-section of a tree was unoccupied against one of the rough stone walls, and ahead was the reception desk. One lamp on either end of it was the only light in the room, but it was enough to make out the features of the man on duty—the two horns poking out of his nest of dark curly hair, his almond eyes, and bulbous nose that was currently pointing downward at an open book.

He looked up at the newcomers and took his time letting his gaze wash over them. Then he grunted, adjusted his cream-colored linen shirt, and got to his feet. Well, in a matter of speaking. Bloom heard the faun's hooves clip-clop against the stone floor. "What can I help you with, Sheriff?"

"We're just here to meet some friends..." She looked around for a name plate of some sort, but found nothing. Apart from the two lamps, the desk only appeared to hold an aged leather guestbook and a brass handbell. "I didn't get your name."

"Galvin. Do your *friends* know you're coming to see them? I prefer for my guests to not have to worry about unexpected visitors."

"I bet you do," mumbled Bloom. "They don't know to expect me. But maybe you can send word ahead." A group of actors was unlikely a flight risk. No doubt they would relish the opportunity to put on a show for her and Ruby.

"Their names?"

"I don't actually know their names," she said. "But I'm sure you noticed them. They're actors."

Galvin grunted again. "Oh yeah. I noticed them, all right. They're the kind that likes to be noticed."

"That's their profession, yes. Will you send word for us?"

He shook his head, and for a moment Bloom feared that this might get ugly. But then he said, "No need. I don't care much for them. Too noisy. Draw too many eyes. And if they never bring their business back here again, I wouldn't shed a tear."

"And you do seem like the weepy type," Ruby interjected, "so I'll take that to mean quite a bit."

He narrowed his eyes at the Fifth Wind, and for a fraction of a second, Bloom could have sworn he was about to grin. "Rooms eleven, thirteen, and fifteen. I think the ringleader is staying in eleven, though, if it's her you want to speak with."

"Perfect," Bloom said. "Thank you so much for your help. I won't forget it."

The staircase was to the right of the desk, and as they moved toward it, Galvin said, "Hound stays down here. No pets."

Bloom said, "Not a chance. He's coming with us," and the matter was all but settled. Galvin could be tough as nails, but no one in their right mind would choose that particular battle against a hellhound, a Fifth Wind, and an angel. And while Galvin was unhelpful at best and an outright criminal at worst, he proved to be in his right mind and let them proceed without argument.

The staircase spiraled upward and was so narrow that they had to go one at a time. Bloom led the way.

Once they reached the landing, iron sconces along the hallway hardly provided enough light to walk without tripping on the uneven floor, so Bloom took it slow as she looked for room eleven.

She shared a quick glance with Ruby, who seemed ready to go, and then she knocked on the thick door.

There was no sound from the other side.

Had they escaped through a window? It wouldn't be hard for fairies. They could simply fly off.

But then the latch moved and as soon as the door cracked open, a torrent of singing rushed out of the room, echoing through the corridor.

A tiny fairy with plump cherry lips and cerulean wings peeked out, realized she'd under judged the height of the guest, and flew a foot higher to be face-to-face with

Bloom. "Hello?" Her eyes darted from one being on her doorstep to the other.

"Hi there. My name's Sheriff Gabby Bloom, and these are my friends Ruby and Clifford. We were wondering if we could have a word with you and the rest of your troop."

The fairy looked on the cusp of refusing, but then her shoulders relaxed, and she pulled the door open wider. "Of course, sheriff. Come on in."

Chapter Thirteen

Ruby True didn't need a nose like Clifford's to be absolutely accosted by the wall of incense burning within the hotel room. What other smells were they covering?

Never mind, she thought. *Better not to know.*

She was pleased to discover that her initial guess on the fairy's lip color, the one she'd made while looking at the black and white flyer int he Pixie Mixie, had proven correct. And that same fairy led them into the cramped room where it appeared the whole troop had gathered to celebrate their performance.

Not one of them, as she scanned their small round faces, seemed particularly pleased to find a sheriff and hellhound suddenly in their presence, and the riotous singing came to an abrupt end. One of them even went so far as to throw the back of her hand to her forehead and pretend to faint out of the air, falling onto the mattress beneath her.

Actors.

Ruby didn't know any fairies personally, but they were simple enough to tell apart from pixies. Both had delicate wings, but a pixie's were opalescent and nearly translucent like a soap bubble, while a fairy's had a distinct coloration that varied from one to the next. There was also an obvious distinction in their bodies. While pixies had humanlike proportions, fairies' bodies were more compact, and their faces had a slight bug-like quality. Nothing Ruby could ever put her fingers on, but something around the eyes.

She'd never seen one with lips like the troop leader's, though. Did fairies get cosmetic surgery? She was relatively sure such a service didn't exist in Eastwind, magical or otherwise. But if this was a traveling band of players, they could have easily found somewhere in Avalon or one of the many connecting realms to it.

"Friends," announced the ruby-lipped woman, puffing her up chest and beginning her monologue, "we have some new guests. As you can see, one of them is law enforcement, and as we have nothing to hide, we will give her our full cooperation. As you know, two catastrophes have befallen our wonderful audience during our last two glorious triumphs of the theater, and it is only natural that those in charge of keeping the peace and protecting the populous would wish to speak with us, as the occurrences do seem strangely related." She nodded, and turned to address Bloom directly. "My name is Bitania Flutterwings"—a stage name if Ruby had ever heard one—"and this is my talented troop of stage performers, the Rambling Mummers." She made a grand sweeping gesture to encompass them.

Most of the fluttering had stopped, and the actors,

who were now perched in various places around the room—the bed, a small writing desk, the accompanying chair—all took a bow at once.

What, did they expect her to clap? Not a chance. Ruby was not a clapper on the whole.

"Rambling Mummers," said Bloom casually, though Ruby knew Bloom rarely did anything casually when she was interviewing people of interest. "An apparent contradiction."

Bitania guffawed. "Indeed it is! Indeed is it! Oh, you're a smart one, aren't you Sheriff Baum? Nothing gets past you, I can already tell! I pity the petty criminal of Eastwind!"

Neither Ruby nor Bloom bothered correcting her on the name.

"This one's a real piece of work," Clifford said.

"I don't need a nose like yours to smell the unicorn swirls all over this room."

"No amount of incense could cover up that *stench."*

"May we have a seat?" Bloom asked.

"Oh! Of course!" crowed Bitania. "Where are my manners? Yes, yes. Take that trunk over there. And here" —she flew over and roughly shoved a turquoise-winged fairy off the desk chair—"this is for you." She smiled at Ruby.

Once they were settled, with Bitania perched on a bedpost at the foot of the bed across from her new audience of three, Ruby did what she preferred to do, which was let Bloom do all the talking while she invited her Insight to come forth and help her keep an eye out for any strange behavior.

Unfortunately, all the behavior in this cramped space

was strange, and Ruby couldn't tell how much was attributable to their being *artists* and how much was downright fishy.

"How long have you been in town?" Bloom began.

"Six days now," Bitania replied.

"And are you enjoying your stay?" She smiled warmly.

The question was perfect. The fairies were clearly settling in for an interrogation, and the unnecessary hospitality was a quick change of direction. Ruby observed the facades around the room crack for just a brief moment. Well, except for the fairy who'd just been knocked off the chair. He'd managed to catch himself right before he hit the ground and had fluttered to a position on one of the pillows, about as far from Bitania as he could be. Bloom's pleasant inquiry hadn't wiped the scowl from his face. In fact, all it resulted in was him crossing his arms. Ruby could hardly fault him for being sour after such treatment.

"Oh *yes*! It's been so wonderful," proclaimed Bitania. "Everyone here is incredibly welcoming, and the town is just so quaint. If I didn't know better than to overstay my welcome, I might settle down here for good."

The fairies behind her bobbed their overlarge heads amicably.

What a load of swirls.

Ruby didn't need to tap into her Insight to know that.

"That's wonderful to hear," Bloom said. "And of course you're welcome to come back whenever you would like. Your production has caused quite a stir around town. I haven't gotten a chance to see it myself, but I hear it's getting rave reviews."

If the sheriff's strategy was to adulate Bitania into submission, she was going about it the right way.

The fairy played bashful in a way that might have appeared subtle to someone fifty yards away. But up close, it just seemed clownish. "I do hope the town appreciates all the hard work we've put into preparing. We really pour our hearts and souls into our work. At times, we even bleed for the love of our art." She added hastily, "Not intentionally, of course, but long hours and grueling emotional scenes do take a toll, and that can lead to accidents."

She looked like she might go on providing examples or simply emphasizing their commitment to their profession, but Bloom stepped in. Ruby wasn't upset about that.

"It's unfortunate that your play has been interrupted in such a way both times. But it speaks to the quality that an audience would stick around for the ending after such a tragedy."

Bitania folded her hands in her lap, staring down at them. "Yes," she said softly. "It's hard to believe that's happened twice. We have our finale in two days' time, and then we move on." She looked up at the sheriff. "I don't mean to sound superstitious, but it docs seem like your townsfolk like to jump from that clock during our productions. Can I assume you'll be keeping a closer eye on it for our Saturday show?"

Bloom leaned back on the sturdy trunk where she sat. "We're keeping an eye on lots of things after this second attempt. We don't intend to let it happen a third time." She paused. "Speaking of which, I do have a question, and I believe your theatrical mind might help me shape this story a bit."

Bitania perked up and a few of the fairies behind her fluttered their wings eagerly. "I do have a theatrical mind."

"We've encountered a problem while investigating this case. No one we've interviewed has actually seen either elf fall. They were all far too engrossed in your dramatic retelling at the time."

"We *are* very captivating," said a small male fairy with butter-yellow wings and bushy eyebrows who was perched on the bed behind Bitania.

The troop leader whirled on him and hissed, "You don't speak!" before returning her attention to Bloom with a dreamy smile already plastered on her face.

Bloom did of good job of pretending not to notice the tension and went on. "So that got me thinking, who *would* have seen the jumpers? Well, we saw the second one."

One of Bitania's little hands flew up to her heart. "And thank *goddess* for that!"

"Right," said Bloom. "Many thanks to the goddess. But I also wonder if anyone on stage might have seen the first jumper."

It wasn't lost on Ruby that Bloom was referring to Bron Danann and Dalora Greyborn as "jumpers" rather than "victims" in front of these fairies of interest. Take away the potential of suspicion, and it was simply trying to make sense of a terrible tragedy—not investigating a possible murder.

"I did," Bitania said, her eyes turning red and welling up in an instant. "It was *horrible*."

Bloom's eyebrows raised. "You saw it? Can you tell me what happened?"

Ruby braced herself for another monologue.

But, despite Bloom having set up the melodramatic troop leader for the perfect moment to let her acting chops shine, Bitania simply replied, "Not much to tell. As I stared out over the transfixed audience, movement behind them caught my eye. I looked up just in time to watch that man drop like a sack of turnips."

"And what time was that?" Bloom asked.

"It was right at noon. The last of the bells was still resonating through the air as he fell. I remember it so vividly. The horror plays over and over again in my mind."

Ruby worried the effort to keep her mouth shut about the time discrepancy might cause her to have a stroke. Bitania was claiming she'd seen Bron fall at noon, but it wasn't until at least ten minutes later that Ted even noticed the body. She wanted to ask why, *why* Bitania hadn't immediately told someone about what she'd seen, but she knew better than to do so. There was no way to phrase it so that it didn't sound accusatory, and she doubted she would receive a sufficient explanation anyway, because as far as she was concerned, one did not exist.

But she could keep her mouth shut no longer, so she jumped in with a different time-related question. "Why start at eleven fifty?"

Bloom had her mouth open, about to ask another question, but she shut it and nodded for Bitania to focus on Ruby's question instead.

Whatever psychological trauma the fairy had been

confronting a moment before at her recollection of the incident vanished. She seemed excited to answer this question, almost as if she'd been waiting for it.

"Ah, that's one of The Rambling Mummers' most well-known flourishes! Whenever we move to a new location, we like to incorporate some of the natural elements of that location into the production. It makes the audience feel like they're a part of the world we're creating!"

"And what did you use for Eastwind?"

He arms flew into the air as she proclaimed, "The bells, of course! Welling here"—she nodded to the disgruntled fairy she'd knocked off the chair—"scouted the area long before we moved our troop in. He said there was an absolutely *divine* location that had the space we needed for our stage and a glorious bell tower that we could use as a sound effect for the thrilling inciting incident of the production."

"Forgive me," Ruby said, "but I haven't had a chance to see the play yet. It involves bells?"

"Oh yes! We've timed it so that it falls perfectly in line with the moment when Queen Naifa's guards, after leading her up to the highest tower in the castle as a means of protecting her, hear the bells of victory sounding from below." She waved her hands and if to wipe away the imaginary painting her words had created. "Oh, I should explain what lead up to that. A mighty rebellion had erupted and Queen Naifa had deployed all of her bravest men, save her personal guards, to strike it down."

Ruby struggled to follow along. "So the queen hears

the bells and they tell her she's safe, that the rebellion has been squashed?"

Bitania shared a knowing look with the fairy closest to her and chuckled patronizingly. "Oh no, no, no. The queen only *thinks* she's safe. But the guards know better. The bells are a signal from the rebels that the rest of the court and the leaders of the queen's army have all been taken or killed. And it is in that moment, as the bells continue to ring in the rebel victory that the queen's guards reveal their true allegiance. They've been traitors the whole time! They kill the queen in that tower, and then parade her body through town."

Ruby cringed. "That's all in the first ten minutes of the play?"

Bitania beamed. "We like to capture the audience's attention from the moment the curtain opens. It's part of why we're so highly reviewed by even the harshest of critics."

"And the rest of the play is about...?" She couldn't imagine where it would go from there that would be of any interest. Already it didn't sound like a book she would read.

"The power vacuum left behind, of course," supplied Bitania. "Lots of scheming and plotting, and even a few duels!"

Ruby snuck a glance at Bloom, and to her dismay, the angel's eyes were large as she leaned forward, taking in every word of the plot with a disarming enthusiasm.

"That's brilliant," said the sheriff. "You take the usual structure and flip it on its head!"

"Indeed!" Bitania nodded appreciatively at the recognition. "I wrote the script myself."

The disgruntled fairy behind her cleared his throat.

"Oh," Bitania added begrudgingly, "and Welling helped with some of the historical research, but only a little."

The gargantuan size of the troop leader's ego was beginning to make Ruby feel claustrophobic in the space.

"And in the scene that takes place in the tallest tower," the Fifth Wind said, "which of you are present on stage in that moment?"

"All of us," the troop leader said. "We aimed to create a sense of total chaos to overwhelm the audience and make them feel like they're present in the kingdom at that moment. So, those of us who aren't immediately involved in the drama are battling on each side of the stage leading up to the ringing of the bells. And then the queen's loyal generals are all either killed or surrender. In that moment all of the frenzied movement freezes on each side, and at center stage, our captive audience beholds the treacherous slaying of the queen."

Bloom nodded along. "Brilliant. Not only do you create a sense of chaos, but when it stops, you create a frame and throw focus to the first turning point of the story."

Ruby glanced at Clifford who looked equally as confused by the Sheriff's sudden enthusiasm, and he tilted his head left and right.

When Bloom locked eyes on the Fifth Wind's skeptical expression, she said, "What? Okay, fine, you got me. I used to be a bit of an actor myself."

"*Really?*" Bitania said, her buglike eyes growing even larger.

Bloom appeared uncharacteristically bashful. "Well, yes. There wasn't much else to do in Heaven to pass the time. Theater is alive and well up there. Of course, they prefer moralistic productions. The scripts have to be approved through a tedious bureaucratic process to make sure the message aligns with the shared beliefs of the ruling angels. Many of the plays feel more like propaganda than art, but still, I found ways to weave genuine emotion into it."

"Perhaps our troop ought to perform in Heaven next!" Bitania turned to the rest of the fairies who fluttered up and down momentarily in excitement.

"Oh yes!" Bloom practically cried. "And you can get up there because you have wings!"

This had certainly taken an unexpected turn, and Ruby was fairly certain that if they wanted to return to some of their main points of questioning, the responsibility for doing so fell squarely on her shoulders.

She cleared her throat. It took doing it twice before anyone noticed. But when they did, she addressed Bitania. "Why didn't you come forward to law enforcement right after the incident? You say you were all present on stage, so even if we discovered that Bron Danann and Dalora Greyborn were both, say, pushed, none of you could be implicated. You all have alibis."

The lead fairy pressed her plump lips together and turned her gaze to the floor. "We were, um, afraid."

"Afraid?" said Ruby.

"Yes. We aren't exactly in town, um..." Her attention turned to Bloom. "Oh, I hope you won't arrest us for this. But we don't have the proper signatures to work in this particular realm. The process takes so long, and it's quite cost prohibitive for our group. Please don't deport us!"

Bloom waved that off casually. "I wouldn't. People come and go from Eastwind plenty. It's impossible to keep track of everyone even if they *do* file the correct paperwork. Those applications have to go through the Parchment Catacombs, and more often than not, they get lost forever."

"I know many places aren't kind to outsiders," Bitania went on.

"True. And if you *do* go up to Heaven," Bloom replied, "I suggest you follow the appropriate protocol for entry. They care about that sort of thing. But down here... Well, most of our problems are caused by the people who were born and raised here."

Bitania nodded, but didn't appear entirely assured.

It seemed to Ruby like the perfect opportunity to escape, so she stood quickly before conversation could pick up again. Even Bloom looked momentarily taken aback by the abrupt move, but she adjusted quickly and got to her feet as well.

Bloom and Ruby said their goodbyes and promised to catch the final show the following Saturday.

And then the angel, the psychic, and the hellhound departed the Ram's Head Inn.

Ruby waited until they were a safe distance away from the Outskirts before voicing her burning suspicion. "They have something to do with it."

Bloom chuckled. "I couldn't agree more. I'll speak with Magnus Taerwyn tomorrow and let you know what he says." After the courtesy and enthusiasm Bloom had shown in the hotel room, Ruby thought they would disagree, but perhaps she'd simply underestimated the angel's acting chops.

Bloom said, "See you at the Emporium on Saturday at around, oh, eleven fifty?"

Ruby grinned. "It's a date."

Chapter Fourteen

Ruby knew it was a dream, but that wouldn't stop her from indulging it. She and Ezra were lying on their backs in the grass just outside Erin Park as unicorns grazed in a nearby pasture. The sun was setting and lit the sky with a burst of tropical colors. They were young again. Well, *she* was young again. Or maybe in this world, she'd never aged, she'd chosen differently, chosen a life with him.

But how long would it last? What would be the cost?

She found that she didn't care. After all, it was a dream. She could indulge this deep fantasy thoroughly now and think about consequences later.

"Ruby," he said from beside her, and she found that they were holding hands. Wasn't that just delightful?

She turned her head to face him, feeling the soft grass caress her cheek. "Yes?"

He sat up suddenly, and she did the same, though with a bit less urgency, keeping her gaze locked onto his.

The sky overhead went dark, and his eyes grew large and urgent. "You have to go."

"What?"

"You have to go!"

"No, I want to stay here a little longer."

"No! You have to wake up. Go *now!*" On the last word, he pressed a hand to each of her shoulders and shoved her hard. The moment the back of her head hit the ground, her eyes shot open and she was back in her bedroom.

Thick malevolence crashed into her like a tidal wave a moment before the spirit at the foot of her bed lunged for her.

She hardly had time to react before the woman's fingers were around her throat. And to Ruby's horror, the fingers had a solidness to them. Not completely, but enough to cause much distress to her windpipe.

Ruby coughed, gasped for air, tried to fight the entity, but each attempt proved futile as her hands went straight through the ghastly apparition. How was this possible? But there was no time for questions now.

She had to find a way to banish this thing before she passed out.

She tried to scream, but she couldn't manage the air for it.

The angry entity gnashed her teeth and yelled and grunted as she continued to strangle the life out of her victim. The leering face was so close to hers, it filled Ruby's diminishing field of view. Wide eyes, swollen with a madness, translucent hair whipping around her face like the snakes of Medusa, nostrils flaring with a primal rage.

Ruby's vision tunneled further, and she knew she didn't have much time.

While she couldn't loosen the woman's grasp, she could still move freely around the bed.

She glanced at her bedside table, but found nothing of use. Just last night's empty teacup and a novel. But wait! Didn't she still have an old staurolite pendant in one of the drawers...?

Her limbs felt heavy from the lack of oxygen, and even as she reached for the drawer, she knew she wouldn't make it before the tunnel closed in on her. The screaming of the spirit would be the last thing she'd ever hear. Oh, what a tragedy!

But then another sound cut through.

A growl.

Clifford leaped clear across the bed, crashing into the spirit and managing to pin her in his terrifying jaws.

She screeched and let go of Ruby's throat, and before Clifford's front paws even reached the floor on the other side of the bed, the spirit had vanished.

The room was silent save for Ruby's choppy gasps.

Clifford climbed up onto the mattress and sat next to Ruby, staring down at her. His hackles were still entirely raised. *"Are you okay?"*

She was particularly grateful for the psychic connection between them right now, when speaking felt so impossible. *"Yes. Well, no. But I will be. I just need a moment."*

Clifford gently placed a heavy paw on one of her arms. *"Take your time. I'll be right here."*

She focused on her breathing, trying to slow it, smooth it out. She was still at risk of passing out if she didn't manage to get a steady flow of oxygen back into her brain.

How had that *thing* gotten through her wards? She didn't have as many in her bedroom as she did in the parlor, but she still had plenty. Whatever it was, it was a powerful entity to be able to bypass the protection she had in place and manifest solidly enough to shut off her air supply.

She glanced at the clock on her bedside table. Usually, the strange spiritual occurrences that awoke her from her sleep happened during the three o'clock hour. But to her surprise, it was only a few minutes past midnight.

She stared up at her familiar who kept a close watch on the exterior wall. *"Did you see what it was?"*

"Not clearly," he replied. *"But I think it had wings."*

Chapter Fifteen

It was amazing how a single night of poor sleep could wreck so much havoc on her now that her thirties were a thing of the past. When Ruby had caught sight of herself in the mirror on Friday morning, the bags under her eyes had practically shouted at her. But what could she have done about it? A spirit had attacked her. A strong spirit. A frighteningly strong spirit. She was lucky to have caught a single wink after that.

But with Clifford standing watch, she'd managed to doze off around sunrise, and one hour of sleep was better than none.

She had firmly decided that today wasn't the day to spend any substantial time looking at herself in the mirror. There wasn't a point, anyway. After over forty decades, she knew what she looked like, more or less. And as much as she would have liked it to, jabbing and fretting over her least favorite features hadn't changed them one bit.

After she set out making her morning tea, she found

she was the kind of tired that had no appetite. But she cooked a breakfast of scrambled eggs and sausages anyway; Clifford had earned it.

The hellhound didn't look much worse for the wear, but she knew he would never show it if he did. She couldn't have asked for a more dutiful familiar.

It was as Clifford was licking the last of the grease from the griddle (in all reality, the last drops were probably long gone and he was simply zoning out) when Ruby sat down and wrote out a message to Sheriff Bloom.

But before she sent it off, she paused. As she'd laid awake the night before, the attack and the case with the bell tower were absolutely connected in her mind. But now that she thought about it, she couldn't be sure. After all, she was a psychic medium. Being surrounded by ghosts with grudges was half her job. Just because Clifford had seen wings and the entirety of The Rambling Mummers had wings didn't mean there was some sort of connection. Plenty of perfectly unconnected people of Eastwind had wings. It was a very normal thing to have, statistically speaking.

Should she even bother Bloom with it? Was it simply a distraction from the more important tasks at hand?

She didn't realize Clifford had stopped his obsessive licking until he spoke to her. *"She won't be mad if you tell her more than she needs to know. She will be upset if you keep something important from her."*

"I didn't invite you into my thoughts."

"You didn't have to. I could tell by your body language."

She frowned at him. She could hardly be mad at him

for being observant when that was one of his best qualities.

"Your Insight is always better at night," he went on. *"You don't filter as much, and it can speak to you better. Don't let your conscious mind stamp it out."*

"You think the attack is related to the case?"

"I don't see how it could be. But I know you felt sure of it last night, and that's good enough for me."

It meant a lot to have someone around who could say such things when her own self-doubt began to act up. If she'd had anymore breakfast food, she would have tossed it his way there and then.

Nearly twenty years of having the gift of Insight, and she still doubted that little voice inside of her. How many times would she have to learn the same lesson again?

"You're right, Cliff," she said aloud, folding up the letter. "I don't know why yet, but I do think the two things are related. Thanks for keeping me honest."

Regardless of the possible connection, she had an urgent errand to which she must attend. One that couldn't wait until the next day. Not if she wanted to get a proper night's sleep, which she very, very much did want.

Her tired body felt twice its normal weight as she and Clifford made the walk from her home to Ezra's Magical Outfitters. Her vanity cried out for some makeup before seeing Ezra, but she hadn't owned any since coming to this town. And besides, Ezra had very little room to comment on her aging process when he didn't even have the nerve to embark upon the ungraceful and occasionally humiliating metamorphosis himself.

Ezra greeted her with a grin, as always, from behind

the front desk when she entered his store, and she forced a wan smile and waved.

"What can I help you with today, beautiful?"

She glanced back through the front windows at Clifford, where he'd decided to remain outside. He enjoyed the outdoors more than a shop like Ezra's that suffocated him with magic. If she'd requested it, he'd have been by her side, but he wasn't needed. "Wards. I need more wards."

Ezra's expression became serious as he hurried over. "Something happen?"

"Oh yes, I'd say so. But nothing Cliff and I can't handle."

Mostly Cliff.

He stopped only a few feet from her and the concern in his eyes grew. "Ruby, is that..." He pointed at her neck, and instinctively her hand flew up to cover it.

"What?" she asked. Swirls. She should have looked in a mirror before coming.

"It looks like bruising," he said. "Did someone try to strangle you?"

She took a step back for space. "As I said, it's nothing Cliff and I can't handle."

He took the hint and didn't push, but instead immediately hustled over to one of the shelves in the back and returned with a black-velvet lined tray full of small objects.

She inspected his selection. For all of Ezra's minor moral faults, she could never say he didn't know his magic. There was a small pile of carved wooden beads, each carrying on it a different rune. Beside that ran a rainbow lock from a unicorn's tail, three copper beads, five jet beads, a heavy piece of malachite carved into a pentagram, and what looked very much like a dried crow's foot.

Yes, she could do some great things with that haul.

"Am I missing anything?" he asked.

She considered it. "Do you have any iron charms?"

He grinned despite his lingering concern. "*Do* I?"

He left the tray atop the nearest glass display case, in which his most expensive items were housed, and returned a moment later with a handful of iron objects.

"This one will do nicely," she said, grabbing the large iron railroad spike. "Not the most beautiful of the objects, but I'd like to see her get past it!"

"See... whom?" he asked quietly, as if the low volume meant he could sneak it in past her better judgment to get an honest answer.

"No one. Yes. I'll take all this." She waved her hand over it.

She was already brainstorming the best configurations to hang at her bedroom window as they walked over to the ledger. He pulled out a satin bag for the collection and as he rattled off the name and price of each one, his words appears in the various columns of the ledger's yellowed pages.

Quickly, Ruby realized she might have overspent. "I don't know that I have all the money on me at the moment, but you know I'm good for it if you just want to make a note and I can come back and pay the rest later."

Ezra glanced up at her, the malachite pentacle in his hand. "No."

"No?" Her eyebrows shot up.

"Look at you, Ruby. Your neck is bruised and, I don't

know if you've noticed this, but there's a burst capillary in your left eye. Whatever happened to you last night was serious. I'm not letting you pay for any of this."

"Ezra," she warned.

He shook his head as he said, "I won't hear it, Ruby. Not from you. I'm not exactly hurting for business lately, if you haven't noticed." He put the last of her haul into the satin bag and pulled it closed with the drawstrings. "What's the point of having money if you can't use it on your friends?"

She almost said, "savings for old age," but while he was being so generous, her desire to prod him for his life choices fizzled out.

"Fine," she said. Then she softened her tone, adding, "And thank you."

"One condition," he said.

Of course there was. "And that is?"

"You go straight to the Pixie Mixie after this and you use your money there. I know you wouldn't be caught dead at the healing house for something so minor, but Stella ought to take a look at you."

It was an easy enough condition to agree to, so she did. And once she had her things and had awkwardly thanked Ezra again, she met Clifford out on the sidewalk and told him of their next destination.

"*He's a good man,*" Clifford said.

"*I hate it, but you're right. At least he's good to me. Anyone else, and he might have sensed the desperation and doubled the prices.*"

"*Did you remember to get iron?*"

"*But of course.*"

Chapter Sixteen

Sheriff Bloom had only assigned herself a single stack of paperwork to get through that day, and then she would track down Magnus Taerwyn, the other elf Liberty Freeman had mentioned to Ruby as a possible close friend of Bron Danann. While she didn't have Insight like Ruby, Bloom still had plenty of intuition built off of millennia of data points, and that intuition was telling her that Magnus wasn't in any immediate danger. At least not until the Rambling Mummers' production in the Eastwind Emporium the following day.

The work was moving slowly today, mostly because the letter she'd received that morning from the Fifth Wind was taking up much of her mental space. Ruby had been attacked. Outside of that fact, little of what she'd mentioned made any sense to Bloom. And then the already confounding letter had concluded with, *Don't worry too much about it, though. I just thought I'd mention in case it had anything to do with our ongoing investigation. I don't see yet how it would, outside of the possible fairy connection, and I know you can't act upon something that flimsy. Anyhow, Clifford and I have the situation under control, and, truly, there's no need to worry. You have enough on your plate as it is and I'm just fine.*

That much effort put toward downplaying it and reassuring the sheriff that it was fine was as clear of an indicator as anything that the altercation had been severe and significant. Otherwise, why would Ruby have sent the letter in the first place? Bloom hoped the witch was lying low today and tending to her health. Of all the days to stay at home and do nothing but read, this would be a good one.

And now the letter was just one more disparate bit of debris knocking around Bloom's mind as she tried to stitch together a coherent theory about Bran and Dalora. There had to be something tying them all together. Some reason why each of the elves were present for one of the performances, why both had decided to climb the long stairs of the tower to the top, and why they had ultimately, whether with help or without, stepped over the edge.

Protesting the play, perhaps? No. That didn't make sense. No one was less enthusiastic about the new local theater scene than Ruby, and she wouldn't even be bothered to protest it.

The berry stains were another anomaly she couldn't connect. There was Ed Willow's fruit stand just near the clock tower. Was it a matter of convenience, then, or did using berries rather than some other substance have a significance? Ruby had sarcastically suggested that Ed might be a person of interest and should be interviewed, and if the talk with Magnus she already had planned for later in the day didn't provide any useful information, she might find herself resorting to that. Ed would, of course, be accommodating, as he always was, but it would ultimately be a waste of time. She could feel that in her gut.

The most persistent question she kept coming back to, the one that would help direct her investigation the most decisively, was the one she just couldn't find an answer to: did the elves jump of their own accord, or were they pushed? Or perhaps they were manipulated. That *was* one of the things Dalora's memory loss hinted strongly at. But only one. There could be a purely medical reason for why her mind had taken an eraser to the moments leading up to the traumatic plunge.

There was no evidence or eye-witness testimony to support that either of the elves had been pushed. No one, as far as she'd heard, had seen anyone else up there. Not even Ruby.

A quick knock, and then the door to her office opened and Deputy Titterfield stuck his head in. "Someone here to see you, Sheriff. He seems pretty distraught. Says he has important information about the clock tower case."

"Thank you, Deputy. Send him right in!"

In the moments that followed, her mind raced with the possibilities of who it could be. Titterfield said "he" but he didn't name him, which meant the deputy didn't know the man's name.

Before her mind could reach any conclusion, the door opened again, and in came a tall man with silky strawberry blond hair down to his waist.

It was an elf if she ever saw one. And she surmised

that she could cancel her plans for the rest of the morning. She no longer needed to track down Magnus Taerwyn.

Because he'd just walked into her office.

"Magnus, I presume?"

His posture froze like she'd just shot him with an ice charm. "Yes. I didn't think you'd know my name. I— I've never been in trouble with the law."

She gestured to the open chair across the desk from her, and he settled himself in it while she cleared the stacks of forms neatly into the corner of her office with a flick of her wrist. "It was only a guess," she said, settling back down into her own seat. "What can I help you with?"

He blanched slightly before launching into it. His oak-colored eyes were overlarge, and dark patches uncharacteristic for his kind formed half-moons below his bottom lashes. "Bron and Dalora. They're my friends. Were my friends. Well, I guess he *was* my friend and she still *is* my friend."

He was clearly nervous. Though he held himself with the same basic dignity expected of elves and kept his spine straight, he wrung his hands in his lap as he struggled to find the proper verb tense for his unfortunate situation.

Bloom already had questions prepared for him for when she sought him out later that day, but she thought it best to simply wait and let him speak. He clearly came here for the express purpose of talking.

"I just... I know this might sound paranoid, but I believe I might be next."

She inspected him carefully. "Next for what?"

"Jumping off the clock tower!"

She nodded. "If you're worried about it, might I suggest not doing it?"

"That's just it! I don't know if I can resist! Bron had a good life. I never had any indication that he would do something like that. He can't have done it himself! He just can't've. Maybe someone was blackmailing him. Or he was hypnotized. Anything! It just wasn't him." He took a deep breath. "As soon as I'd heard about it, I knew something wasn't right. And Dalora..." He paused again, and Bloom caught a hint of deep history there. "Never. No, never."

"You don't believe she would do it either?"

He shook his head divisively. For all his insecurity, he did seem sure about that. "Whatever happened to Bron happened to her. That seems obvious. They went in the exact same way."

Bloom narrowed her eyes and decided to risk it. "Did you hear anything about a stain on her shirt?"

Magnus's smooth skin wrinkled at the corners of his eyes. "What do you mean? A stain? I don't know anything about that."

In that case, far be it from Bloom to taint the source. She folded her hands and set them on her desk. "I know it's all very hard to understand when things like this happen, Mr. Taerwyn. Thankfully, Dalora is okay and should be released from the healing house soon. But you should know that it's not uncommon for those close to someone who dies at their own hand to copy the behavior shortly after."

He blinked. "I don't follow your meaning."

She hated to do this, but sometimes the best way to

squeeze all the relevant information from a person was not to ask directly, but to antagonize just enough. "I mean, I've seen situations before where someone within a community tragically takes his or her own life. And shortly after, one or more of those closest to the deceased duplicate the act, mimicking the details to the letter. I don't claim to understand it, but my best guess, if I had to make one, is that the reenactment is a way of reconnecting with the one they've lost, of trying to see things from their loved one's eyes, maybe answer some of the same questions. Or perhaps they fear that if someone they loved and respected lost hope that means there is no hope for anyone." She leaned back in her chair and kicked her legs out beneath her desk. "I'm here to assure you that there is *always* hope. And I speak from a place of experience. I've seen it time and again. In the moments when life seems most hopeless, that's where the deepest and richest wells of it can be found." She paused. "You're not here to provide information, are you?"

Her implications about his friends had rattled him enough, it seemed, because when he spoke, it was with a thinly veiled fury. "No. I have no information to give you, *especially* if you're looking for evidence that my two friends attempted to take their own lives. They would never do that."

"What do you really believe happened, then? Pretend I don't need evidence to believe it and act upon it. What is your gut telling you?"

"That Bron was murdered, and whoever forced him off the edge also attempted to murder Dalora. And I believe whoever did it is going to do the same to me!" His chin quivered and he lowered his voice to hardly more than a whisper. "Please, sheriff. I need your protection."

"Who do you believe would want to murder you and your friends?"

His eyes lowered to his hands as he said, "I don't know." He met her stare again. "But you know as well as I do that if you live long enough, you amass enemies."

"How long have you been alive?"

"Just over four hundred years."

She nodded. "You're old, even for your kind. And your friends?"

"Just about the same."

She sighed. "You're right, that's plenty of time to rub a few people the wrong way. But generally speaking, who have you rubbed wrongly enough that you now fear lethal retribution?"

He answered without hesitation. "No one."

But with his words came a flash of warm, pulsating guilt that shot off of him and hit her square in the chest. She didn't even have to gaze inside him to find it.

Did she think he would tell her the cause of it? Not a chance.

"Well, Mr. Taerwyn, I hear your concerns. And I would love to provide you with, for lack of a better phrase, round-the-clock security. But as you may or may not know, the High Council only supplies us with enough funds to employ myself, Deputy Titterfield, and part-time help at the front desk. We don't have a body to spare." She paused, inspecting the genuine fear in his eyes. That, at least, wasn't a lie. "For what it's worth, I have no reason to believe you are in any grave danger at the moment. What I suggest is that you stay away from the Emporium for at least a week. If you're concerned about replicating the scene, don't provide an opportunity for it. Simple as that. And do stay calm. I know you're going through a period of great mourning for your friend. Take time to experience that pain. I promise it doesn't last forever. It's simply a dark tunnel through which one must pass."

"Don't lecture me about loss," he snapped.

She didn't flinch a muscle. Instead, she merely thought, *Well, isn't that interesting?* "I don't mean to lecture. But dealing with loss is a lesson one must learn over and over again."

"And I have," he said. "Over and over and over again! All due respect, Sheriff, but you don't know anything about me and what I've been through. You come from Heaven, so perhaps you're a little ignorant to the way things work outside of Heaven and Eastwind, but let me tell you, sometimes it's nothing *but* loss, nothing *but* pain." He stood. "If you can't offer me a single bit of protection, then I'm done sticking around and listening to your patronizing advice. There are a million other things I'd rather do with my time. Or what's left of it."

Even though his sudden rage was disarming, she knew better than to say another word to him. When the fire was raging like this in another, all words became tinder, no matter the intent behind them.

He slammed the door behind him, and she waited until she heard the exterior doors of the station slam as well before getting up from her desk.

As she stepped into the hall, Deputy Titterfield poked his head out of his office to check on the commotion, and Bloom smiled. "Don't worry, Morris. You're not needed at this moment."

She made straight for the front desk, where their receptionist wouldn't be arriving for another few hours, and grabbed a slip of owl parchment and a pen. She wrote the letter in her clearest cursive, and folded it up, sealing it with the wax stamp of the Sheriff's Department crest. And then on the front, she wrote the recipient's name: *Stu Manchester*.

The boy would be released from Mancer Academy for the weekend in a matter of hours. And she doubted he would mind the homework she was assigning him.

Chapter Seventeen

The bell above the front door of the Pixie Mixie Apothecary jingled, and Ruby's Insight gave her another swift kick in the seat of her pants.

I know, she told it. *I heard you the first time.*

Ruby asked Kayleigh if she could speak with Stella, and one look at Ruby was enough for the store's owner to stop her shelving and hurry to it.

"*I don't look* that *bad, do I?*" She looked down at Clifford.

His tail, which had been lazily wagging at the sight of Kayleigh, dropped like stone. "*No. Of course not.*"

"*You're a terrible liar. But thanks for trying.*"

A moment later, Stella Lytefoot fluttered out of the back room of the Pixie Mixie. She had brown hair so dark it flirted with being black, and while she was equally as beautiful as her partner, her features were much more defined, almost severe. Her sharp nose appeared chiseled from marble, and her dark eyes carried a nonstop intensity in them.

Part of that might have been due to the fact that Stella's mind had a nonstop intensity to it. She was a master of potions and a top candidate for Eastwind's Most Brilliant.

She was not, however, a contender for Eastwind's Most Tactful.

"Who strangled you?" she asked by way of greeting.

Kayleigh groaned and returned to her inventory.

"Not sure. But Ezra insisted I come see you and get a little treatment for it."

"He was right, telling you to do that. Follow me."

Ruby and Clifford did, and they quickly found themselves in the back office of the Pixie Mixie where Stella was reported to spend most of her waking hours and many of her sleeping ones, as well. The walls of the windowless room were lined with shelves that held jars and bottles of all shapes and sizes with contents just as varied. Almost none were labeled from what Ruby could tell, and those that were simply had small signs below them that said things like, *very deadly* and *mostly deadly,* and *nope, not this one.*

"Have a seat," Stella said, motioning to a chair at the long stone table that ran down the center of the space.

As Ruby complied, Stella popped the lid off a wooden container on the top shelf, reached her small hand inside, and pulled out a bone with dried bits of muscle and tissue still clinging to it.

Ruby was already readying herself to politely say no thanks, when Stella asked, "Can he have it?"

Clifford wagged his tail, scenting the air like mad in the direction of the bone.

"What is it?" Ruby asked. Obviously, it was a bone. But different animal's bones had different properties.

Stella didn't appear offended by the question. "Jackalope," she replied. "Chewing it will create a slight feeling of euphoria for him."

"You mean more than chewing bones usually does?" She looked at her familiar and didn't miss the drool already pooling at the corners of his jowls. "Yes, that's fine." She patted his head. "He's earned it today."

Stella tossed him the bone and he snatched it out of the air. "Did he help fight off your attacker?"

"He did."

The pixie nodded promptly then zipped over to another shelf where she began rooting through different containers, gathering various ingredients in her arms. "You said you didn't know who it was. How is that possible?"

"She woke me from my sleep. She was in my face before I could do much, and I didn't recognize her. Clifford said she had wings, though."

Stella set the last of the ingredients down on the table and began sprinkling them one by one into a large cast-iron cauldron.

"You can touch iron?" Ruby asked. "I thought all fae avoided it."

"We do. It's painful, like if you touched a hot pan on the stove. But a bit of accidental contact here and there is worth it for me. Besides, it's not *that* painful for pixies. Not sure why, but we're not as sensitive to it. Fairies, though... phew, they do *not* like it."

"What about elves?"

Stella sprinkled something white into the mixture

that looked and smelled a bit like goat cheese but made a distinct farting noise the second it touched the other ingredients. "Elves pretend iron doesn't affect them, and then they subtly avoid it. I couldn't honestly tell you how much it repels them because they're too *dignified* to talk about it. Even for posterity. Trust me. I've asked."

"You don't sound like a fan of elves."

"I don't have to be," she said dryly. "They're a big enough fan of themselves."

Ruby enjoyed Stella's conversation very much. But then again, she always did love a straight shooter.

"What else can you tell me about your attacker?" the pixie prompted.

"It was a spirit."

Stella's thin lips parted as her mouth popped into a small O. Her concoction was temporarily forgotten as she stared up at Ruby in amazement. "A spirit was able to grab you and do this much damage?"

"Yes," Ruby said, "I was surprised, too."

"Is that usual?"

"No. But it's not unheard of with the highly powerful ones. And she wasn't able to grab me completely, just enough to cut off my air."

"Did you pass out?" Stella didn't even blink as she asked the question, and Ruby found herself feeling more like a science experiment than a witch.

"No."

"I'm surprised to hear that. You look like a mess. I'd have expected you to have passed out."

Ah, so that bluntness wasn't *always* her friend. "I was very close to it. Clifford scared her off before that happened."

"You said you were speaking with Ezra earlier." She returned to her mixture, grabbing a large pestle and mashing furiously. "Should I take that to mean you're going to be warding your room better later?"

"Indeed."

Stella crushed something that looked like dried dung into the cauldron and said, "Could this attack have anything to do with the elves jumping to their deaths?"

She wasn't sure how Stella's mind had made it there, but she had no problem being honest. "I believe so. And only one actually died. Bloom managed to save the other." If she was looking for relief from the pixie, she was looking in the wrong place.

"Do you think you're being targeted for your involvement in investigating it?"

"That I don't know." Ruby *was* being targeted, though, wasn't she? The berry stains. Were they singling her out? She wasn't sure what else "5th" could pertain to.

But wait. She had the most brilliant mind in Eastwind at her disposal right now. Might as well put it to the test.

"There was something peculiar about both of the jumpers."

"Outside of normal elven behavior?"

"Yes." Ruby paused. "Both had something written on their shirts."

She was pleased to see that the tidbit had caught Stella's interest as the pixie looked up from her work. "What was it?"

"The word '*5th.*'"

Stella considered it for a moment and then nodded once before tapping the pestle on the side of the cauldron. A peach-colored goo slid off of it and into the bowl. "That makes sense."

"It does?"

She grabbed a thick cinnamon stick from the table and used that to stir the mix now. "Yes. I mean, it doesn't completely make sense, but there's a connection."

"Okay. And that connection is...?"

"The play, obviously."

"How is the writing on their shirts connected to the play?"

"It's a story about the events following the betrayal of Queen Naifa, isn't it?"

"That's what I've heard, yes."

"She wasn't the first of her name. No, no. I remember a few of the others. They were equally rubbish at ruling."

Ruby considered it. "Are you telling me that the play is about Queen Naifa *the Fifth?* That's what you believe *5th* relates to?"

Stella shrugged. "Seems pretty obvious, right? Now, why someone would write that on their clothes and jump off a clock tower, that's something I'll leave up to you and Gabby Bloom to figure out."

Stella dipped her fingers in the paste and pulled out a sizable amount. The mixing had turned it the color of a ripe blueberry. Without delay, the pixie flew over and began covering Ruby's neck with a thick layer of it. The pungent scent, which quickly reached the witch's nostrils, left something to be desired.

So as Stella continued applying it, Ruby decided to lose herself in her mind. The theory Stella had just presented made so much sense. This was all about the play, wasn't it? Bron and Dalora timing their jumps with it—and didn't Bitania say the bells were used for the murder scene?—the stains on their shirt referencing the queen being murdered on stage. It was starting to fall together.

And yet, there remained so many other loose ends to tie up in this snowballing theory, so many more questions to be answered.

And an old line from a play she hadn't thought about in ages surfaced in her mind: *The play's the thing...*

Indeed it was.

Chapter Eighteen

While Ruby wasn't thrilled that she was spending a beautiful Saturday watching community theater, it did help that it was part of a murder investigation.

It also helped that Zax Banderfield had been able to meet her for the show. Ruby had arranged for them to meet with time to spare, and she was glad she had. After a spot of tea at A New Leaf around ten (Harvey Hardtimes clearly hadn't forgotten that Zax had previously stood her up, and the proprietor was keeping a close eye on the werebear), they strolled the Emporium, which was bustling with its usual weekend foot traffic.

Zax had a cool fifteen inches on her height, and she was keenly aware they made a strange match in other ways, physically speaking. She often wondered why he seemed interested in her, with her lack of attention to wardrobe and unintentional statement of fiery curls that seemed to have a mind of their own. She didn't make a practice of disparaging her looks, but she was a realist: there were plenty of better looking women in Eastwind who would jump all over a muscular man like him, with his ocean-blue eyes, thick chocolate hair sun-streaked with copper, and a strong nose that could have been sculpted by the hand of an Italian Master. And that didn't even touch upon the power he wielded around town as a member of the High Council and Sleuth Leader of the Eastwind werebears—and everyone knew power could be quite the aphrodisiac for a woman in search of a mate.

But she could easily cast aside those questions whenever she was with him. His attention to her left no room for them. She may never know the answers, but he made it clear that he was in fact interested in her.

"Any news from Fluke Mountain?" Ruby asked as they left a bakery with a fresh baguette and small sausage each. It was Ruby's favorite simple lunch, and the only thing that kept her from eating it every day was her lack of desire to leave the house every day.

Zax pulled off a piece of bread and said, "None that would interest you," before popping it into his mouth.

"Meaning no attacks or murders or ghosts?"

"Precisely."

She feigned offense. "I'm interested in other things than all that."

"Oh yeah?" He grinned down at her. The werebear had a cool foot and a half on her, height wise. "Like what?"

"Well, open-air theater, for one."

He laughed. "Yes, you sounded so excited about it. Am I right in assuming this is more work than pleasure for you?"

"I thought we'd already decided to mix the two."

"I'm not complaining," he said, holding his hands up in surrender, "I'm glad to spend whatever time we can together."

And yet, there was less and less of it lately.

She decided not to dwell on that. She enjoyed any time she could get with the head of the Eastwind werebears. Why complicate it? It was so rare she enjoyed her time with anyone other than Clifford. And, of course, Bloom.

"How are Opal and Cedric?" she asked. "Has their romance endured?"

The two werebears had been involved in a sticky situation after Opal's boyfriend, Swamy, had caught wind of her affair with Cedric Pine.

"Of course not," he said. "Opal's had three other boyfriends since then."

"Three? It's only been a few months."

"Exactly. I'm surprised it isn't more."

"That's awfully judgmental," she chided.

He shrugged and took a bite from his sausage. "Hey, no judgment from me. Just an observation. I remember being young. When I was in my early twenties, I had a different girlfriend each week."

"And now?"

"I prefer quality over quantity."

She nudged him in the side with her shoulder. "Well, I wish you the best finding a quality girlfriend in *this* town."

"I appreciate the support, but I think I might already have my eye on someone who fits the job description."

"Sounds like even *dating* is work for you."

He shrugged. "Maybe so. But I always throw myself into my work. No one's complained yet."

Ruby felt her face redden.

"For what it's worth," she said, trying to change the subject, "I am very interested in the play. I've heard only rave reviews about it."

"Then you and I must not be talking to the same people. I've heard only strange things about it," he replied.

They settled on a small rock wall and Ruby was able to juggle her lunch a little better as they people watched. "What sort of strange things have you heard all the way up on Fluke Mountain?"

"That elves like to jump from there"—he pointed at the top of the clock tower—"in the middle of the play."

"Yes, that *is* a strange feature." She gazed up at the structure. Would there be a third elf standing on the edge in less than an hour? Bloom's correspondence about her meeting with Magnus Taerwyn had been brief and expressed little more than the angel's lack of concern for his safety and that she was taking the necessary precautions to manage it. It was almost as if Bloom were hiding something. From Ruby. But that made no sense.

"I've heard of some wacky performance art," Zax continued, "but never suicide."

"What about homicide?"

He turned quickly to look at her. "You think so?"

"I... have a hunch."

"Your hunches are as good as knowing, far as I'm concerned. Your so-called hunch about Swamy Stormstruck was right. I never would have thought the missing man was also the one behind the attacks."

She grinned up at him. "Which is why it's a good thing this town has me."

He didn't pull his eyes away from her when he said, "If only they realized how lucky they are."

She broke the eye contact hastily. "Yes, well, that's just part of being a beacon for death. Never the life of the party."

They finished the rest of their cheese and bread in silence as they observed the passersby. A few of them waved hello or stopped to chat with Zax, but Ruby's conversational skills weren't called upon even once. It seemed no one made the connection that Ruby and Zax were sitting next to one another on the wall, eating the exact same meal, because they were spending time together. Intentionally. People seemed to regard it as a mere coincidence that he was in the same place at the same time as her, and perhaps he had been sitting on that rock wall and she had impolitely come up and sat down without asking. She could hardly blame anyone for their incorrect assumptions, though. They *did* make an odd couple.

In fact, she wouldn't even call them a couple. Would she?

Stop complicating it.

She finished the last of her food just as a familiar voice boomed over the crowd. Bitania was clearly speaking through magical amplification as she welcomed the audience and introduced herself and her troop.

After wiping the grease off their hands on the soft grass behind them, Ruby and Zax moved closer to the stage. It was crucial she hear every word of the production. There could be good insights buried in the dialogue. And if there was, this was her last chance to hear it.

Zax put his arm around Ruby's shoulder, and she leaned into his large, strong body. Oh, this was nice...

Focus!

But the sunlight and her full stomach were making her sleepy. She knew that she only need ask, and her date would happily accompany her home for a nap... and maybe more. And wouldn't that be a delightful way to spend a weekend afternoon?

Afternoon. After noon. Right. It wasn't even that time yet. It was only eleven fifty.

Bitania disappeared behind the curtains, which opened only a second later. Two of the fairies beat large drums for drama, as two actors fluttered onstage, dressed in flimsy stage armor.

Ruby was already bored.

She scanned the crowd until she located Gabby Bloom. The angel was ten yards behind her, arms crossed over her chest, obviously attempting to present as if she wasn't pleasantly reliving her own glory days on stage up in Heaven.

When Ruby caught her eye, Bloom nodded. Good. The plan was still in place, then.

"Ah, I knew it," spoke Zax in a low tone.

She looked up at him to find he had followed her gaze and was now looking at Bloom as well. He waved to the sheriff.

"It *is* work that brought you here, isn't it?"

"Like you said," she whispered back, "nothing wrong with mixing work and pleasure."

"I don't disagree. But I do wonder which one takes precedence. Am I just a cover for you?"

"Of course not!" she insisted. She placed a hand on his where it remained on her upper arm, holding her close to him. "I'm just glad that work finally allowed me a moment with you."

He nodded, but didn't reply and returned his attention to the stage.

Shoot. The play. How easily she was distracted from something she had no desire to pay attention to in the first place.

Although, she had to admit, the scene where the guards whisked Queen Naifa, played of course by Bitania herself, into the highest tower *was* quite tense. The acting wasn't half bad... for community theater. And when the first bell tolled in Fallia's Eye behind Ruby's back, commencing the brief introduction tune before ringing in the hour, the effect was powerful. She *did* feel like she was there in the tower with the queen.

Relief washed over Bitania's face as the bells rang out the last of the song before counting out the hours.

"Could it mean what I hope?" she proclaimed during the brief pause.

One of the fairy guards said, "It does. It means victory is at hand."

Doooom...

"Thank Mother Earth!" the queen proclaimed again.

Doooom...

One of the guards then added, "You forget to ask *whose* victory, my queen."

Doooom...

A shadow passed between Ruby and the sun, hardly

more than a flicker, and when she glanced up, she saw Sheriff Bloom flying overhead, away from the Emporium, a blur of white and tan.

What the hellhound?

The sheriff was supposed to keep a close eye on the clock tower in case anyone else decided to see if they could fly. But if she was leaving, then who was watching it?

Ruby shielded her eyes from the sun to get a good look at the jumping point. No one was there. But what would she even do if someone was? She couldn't swoop in and catch them like Bloom could. The sheriff had left her completely on her own with no tools to handle the situation.

But as the clock continued to toll and finally ended after the twelfth and final ring, there was still no one to be seen at the top of the clock tower.

And on stage, Queen Naifa V was dead.

Were they in the clear now? Hadn't the last two instances taken place during that particular scene?

Doubt swarmed her like a cloud of gnats. What if the jumpers simply *had* been a coincidence? What if the play actually had nothing to do with it?

But her Insight rejected both of those questions. The events had to be related to the play. But why had no one jumped? She checked again. Still no one visible in the bell tower above the clock face.

Was she *disappointed* by that? No, that would be horrible.

And yet, it would validate a theory that had been growing more solid by the second up until the point when the final bell sounded.

Someone tapped her on the arm, and she jumped and looked around until she spotted the offender.

A young, red-faced boy with intense, beady eyes and copious freckles stared up at her.

"Can I help you?"

"You're Ruby True, right?" he asked.

She could tell by his tone that something was terribly wrong. "Yes. And you're Stu Manchester."

"The Sheriff sent me to get you. She needs you to follow me right away."

Ruby's brow furrowed as she tried to make a decision. Would Bloom really have sent a child to get her, or was this some sort of trap?

"She said you'd be skeptical," he said. "So she told me to tell you that if you don't come, she'll tell everyone about the time you accidentally used thistle instead of fennel in your hair removal potion."

Ruby's eyes shot open, and she quickly checked to make sure Zax hadn't heard that.

It was clear by the amused way he was staring down at Stu that he had.

Well, maybe he wouldn't understand the full implications of what it meant... or how long it took her to remove the bristly beard afterward.

"Fine, fine," she said, "lead the way."

She looked at Zax and nodded for him to follow.

"Sounds like it's suddenly all work and no pleasure," he said, staying put. "I'll leave you to it. Let me know when you're ready to swap those proportions."

Fair enough.

She called to Clifford and then set out through the enraptured crowd, weaving this way and that to follow little Stu Manchester to whatever emergency Bloom had flown to in such a hurry.

"Where are we going?" Ruby asked as they headed entered the Erin Park neighborhood.

"The house of Magnus Taerwyn."

"The elf?"

"Yes, ma'am."

"But doesn't he live in Tearnanock Estates?"

"He does, ma'am."

"And you know about Tearnanock Estates?"

"I do, ma'am."

Her lungs screamed at her to stop wasting her breath on conversation, but her question was too pressing. "*How do you know about it? I thought it was mostly a secret.*"

"It is, ma'am. But Sheriff Bloom told me about it a while ago for a situation such as this."

"And what exactly *is* this situation?"

He stopped in his tracks to look at her straight on. And with a manner of seriousness reserved for boys of his age, he said, "Surveillance."

Really, Gabby! Sending children to keep an eye on persons of interest!

But at the same time, there was a brilliance to it.

Ruby knew very little about Stu Manchester, but his reputation of abiding by and upholding the law preceded him already.

The poor kid was probably bullied something terrible at school.

"Fine then," she said, "lead the way." And a part of her was thrilled. She was going to get to see the invisible avenue of the elves.

Chapter Nineteen

They hurried through Erin Park, Ruby and Clifford following behind Stu Manchester. If this turned out to be a true emergency, they would be poor help. Clifford had no trouble with the speed, but Ruby found herself not quite up for the task of chasing down a boy who could be no older than twelve.

"This way, Ms. True."

They slipped down an allyway between two shops, and a moment later, Stu Manchester reached into seemingly empty space in front of him and grabbed hold of something.

He pulled open the invisible door.

"That's it?" Ruby asked. "Not exactly fantastic security."

Stu held it open for her. On the other side was a staircase that looked only a little less grimy than the alley in which they stood. "Only certain people can open the door," he explained. "The residents, the High Council, and a few other key members of the community."

"And you," Ruby remarked, passing through ahead of him.

"And me. Bloom snuck me on the register so I could spy." His eyes went wide like he'd just been caught with his hand in the cookie jar. "Don't tell anyone I can do this, though!"

Clifford passed the threshold, and Stu closed the invisible door behind him. From this side of it, it was clearly visible—solid wood with an ornately carved copper handle.

"You're secret's safe with me," she assured him.

Up the stairs they went until they were, she guessed, even with the rooftops of the buildings below. She couldn't see the rest of Erin Park, though. Apparently, the Elves didn't want to be reminded of where they actually were. Instead, Ruby found herself in brilliant sunshine in the middle of an achingly green field. Wind tickled the tops of the blades of grass that spread impossibly for miles to her left and right. Whatever magic Liberty Freeman had employed to defy the laws of physics in his own home was in no short supply here. But Ruby didn't have long to appreciate the views. Stu was already jogging down a flagstone road, and she grunted against the pain in her lungs and then hurried to catch up.

The houses came into view suddenly as they turned a bend around a lush copse of trees.

"Houses" seemed like the wrong word, though. They were mansions. Estates.

You're in Tearnanock Estates, stupid.

Right.

Was it possible for her to retire here someday? Could

she get permission? Surely the High Council owed her that, with how much she did to keep the town safe and mostly ghost-free.

Helping solve the mystery of the jumping elves would also be a step in the right direction.

But before she could do that, she had to face whatever strange thing Bloom had waiting for her.

* * *

Fresh air was always the best thing for someone in Magnus's state, so once Sheriff Bloom had done a quick soul-level scan for any bodily injury and come up clean, she led him back out onto his front porch and set him down on a rocking chair. As she continued to ask him basic questions and observe his behavior, she heard the peculiarly deep voice of young Stu Manchester call out to her. "I have her, Sheriff. And her hound."

She turned away from where she'd knelt in front of Magnus, keeping an eye on him, and saw the triplet approach. Stu jogged up the steps to the wrap-around porch and appeared red-faced from exertion but otherwise fine.

Ruby, on the other hand...

Hmm. Bloom hadn't considered what it would require to hurry all the way from the Emporium. She herself had merely taken flight and hit the shortcut in the air, the one she was to use in case of an emergency in Tearnanock. She'd put in the special request with Liberty when he was building the place way back when. She hadn't told any of the current residents that it existed, and she had no plans of doing so.

"Thank you, Stu," Bloom said, pulling her attention away from Ruby, who'd stopped running the moment she'd spotted the sheriff and could see that continuing to hustle was not absolutely necessary. "Here you go." She held out a silver coin, but the boy's hand flew out—to refuse it.

"I can't possible take payment for this, Sheriff Bloom."

Ruby rolled her eyes. "Just take the dragon blasted money, kid."

Not one to ignore a direct order from an adult, Stu complied, but he didn't look happy about it. "Anything else I can do, Sheriff?"

Bloom smiled at him. "Go enjoy your weekend like someone your age should."

He frowned and murmured, "Yes, ma'am," before shuffling off with his head hanging.

"What happened?" Ruby panted, after passing Stu at the bottom of the stairs and taking in the sorry sight of Magnus slumped on the rocking chair.

Magnus opened his mouth to speak, but Bloom placed a hand softly on his shoulder. "Don't worry. You rest and I'll fill her in." She turned to Ruby. "Magnus can't remember what happened. Starting at *noon*."

Ruby's eyebrows shot up her forehead. "Oh yeah? Another missing memory?"

"So it seems."

Ruby pressed her lips together. "I reckon he's safe now. At least until midnight."

"I was thinking the same." Bloom checked on Magnus again, and the fresh air seemed to have done him good already. His chest was rising and falling slowly, and his eyes were able to focus on her when she suggested they get him set up in bed.

He agreed, and when the angel returned to the porch, Ruby was sitting on one of the front steps, looking out over the green expanse.

"Do you sense anything?" Bloom asked.

"Yes, but hardly more than an afterglow. If I could have gotten here sooner, I believe it would be much stronger. Either way, it's familiar."

Oh, *that* was interesting. "Familiar as in...?"

"I believe we're on the same page that we're dealing with possession?"

Bloom took a seat next to Ruby. Clifford was roaming the yard, sniffing all he could. "If that's the page you're on, then yes."

The Fifth Wind turned her head to look Bloom in the eyes. "Did Stu summon you away from the play?"

"He did."

"And how did he manage that?"

Bloom reached in her pocket and pulled out the small, round disk of jet. "Enchanted."

Ruby took one appraising look at it and said, "Let me guess. Ezra?"

The sheriff nodded.

"Allow me another guess. It's not *technically* legal in Eastwind."

"Ah," Bloom said, wagging a finger at her friend, "it's not technically *illegal* either."

Ruby almost smiled. "Leave it to the angel to find all the possible loopholes."

"Please, I know you're impressed."

"And what prompted little innocent, law-abiding Stu

Manchester to employ a device that he likely had no idea isn't technically legal to summon the sheriff at a moment's notice?"

"Oh right." She stood and dusted off the back of her pants. "You haven't been inside yet. Follow me."

She offered Ruby a hand and helped her to her feet, then the two of them entered the giant home.

"It's elegant in here, no doubt," Ruby said as they passed through the foyer, heading to the back of the house. "But I don't see what I'm supposed to get from this."

"Stu Manchester was watching Magnus through the window while the elf prepared himself a salad for lunch. Nothing unusual there. But was *was* notable was when Magnus decided to drag the paring knife for the tomatoes across his palm and so he could redecorate his walls."

"Come again?" said the witch.

They reached the kitchen, and Bloom entered first, but stepped to the side to allow Ruby to pass. It was easier if the Fifth Wind saw this for herself.

It was hard to shock Ruby, but this did it. Her mouth fell open before she breathed, "Sweet... baby... jackalope..."

"Agreed." Even Bloom felt a roiling anxiety when she looked at the walls and counters on which Magnus had written the same thing over and over again: *5th.*

Ruby's head snapped around to Bloom. "Little Stu saw this happen?"

The sheriff cringed guiltily. "Yeah, sort of unfortunate."

"He's going to be scarred for life."

"Probably."

"Might make him a good deputy one day."

"Childhood trauma isn't required, but it's preferred, yes."

Ruby took in the surroundings once more before saying. "It's settled then. My theory holds fast."

"And that is?" She thought she already knew, but she wanted to hear it from Ruby's lips first to verify.

"The entity that caused Bron Danann and Dalora Greyborn to jump from the clock tower, and I do believe it was a single entity influencing them, was the same one who caused Magnus Taerwyn to do a slap-dash kitchen makeover."

"The calling card is definitely the same." Bloom gestured at "5th" on the wall nearest her.

"But more than that," Ruby said, tucking her hands deep into the pockets of the topmost layer of her robes, "I do believe this same entity was the one who attacked me in my bed."

Bloom nodded slowly. "That's where you recognize the after glow from."

"Precisely." She twisted slowly in her spot, looking again over the walls. "Each spirit has a unique energetic pattern. The more malevolent, the more pronounced."

"Why do you think it went after you?" asked Bloom.

"Because I was trying to stop it."

The sheriff shrugged. "I've been doing the same. It didn't go after me."

Ruby nodded. "That's just proof that it's an *intelligent* entity, in more ways than one. Trying to strangle an angel to death is a fool's errand if I ever heard one."

"True," Bloom said. "And I think I already know the answer to this, but *how* did it go after you?"

"The attack happened at midnight."

Nodding along, Bloom said. "Midnight and noon."

"Either the spirit is obsessed with the number twelve, which I feel is highly unlikely since it already seems fixated on the number five, or we have a clear picture of the next location where we must go."

"I don't know about you, but the next place I'm going," said Bloom, "is the healing house with Magnus. I was able to close the wound, but he still lost a lot of blood. Once I take care of that, I'll meet you there. And I'll send word ahead to Mayor Periwinkle in the meantime."

"It's a date," Ruby said. "You, me, Clifford, bottom of the clock tower at, say, two thirty?"

"You're on. Now let's get the everloving hellhound out of this kitchen."

Chapter Twenty

Mayor Petrov Periwinkle was all niceties when they met a couple of hours later, as planned. He'd even bothered to put on a powder blue suit. Sheriff Bloom knew that meant he was hiding something. And when she shook his hand and looked into his eyes, as much was confirmed. She didn't love using her powers of judgment on others without their consent, but she'd make an exception for the insufferable mayor.

Unfortunately, the cause of the guilt he held was unknowable. It could have had something to do with the case, but it also could have had something to do with the myriad shady dealings he managed at any given point in time. Or maybe he had plans to cut funding once and for all to Mancer Academy, forcing every family to pay an insane tuition out of pocket if they wanted their child educated. It wasn't out of the question for him. He was the biggest cheapskate she knew.

Thankfully (and she never thought she would be thankful for the vampire in any way), Count Malavic was the treasurer on the High Council and enjoyed shelling out funds for things... in return for loyalty from the recipients.

As long as children got a proper education in town, though, she wasn't picky on how it was done. The more educated the town, the less work she had on her plate.

Ruby and Cliff stood to Bloom's side as they faced the mayor at the base of the clock tower. The Emporium was still rather busy, as it normally was on a Saturday, even during this time of day when most people chose to return home for a nap.

"I'm not clear on what you're looking for," Mayor Periwinkle said, wringing his hands slowly, "so perhaps if you enlighten me, I can be of more help."

"We'll know it when we see it, Mr. Mayor." Bloom wasn't about to let him within arm's reach of this investigation. She'd made that mistake before, and it'd resulted in the case becoming so entangled in red tape, it'd taken three extra weeks to make an arrest, even though she had plenty of evidence for it. "Otherwise, if you could just answer our questions, that would be extremely helpful."

He frowned. "If there's anything wrong with the structure, we would have known right away."

She could understand why he would be so defensive. After all, not only was the clock a local historical landmark, but it was also one of the hidden entrances into the High Council's chambers below. If the answer was sitting on top of them the whole time... Well, it wouldn't help the politicians' image as complete bumblers.

Good. I hope the answer is not only up there, but gloriously obvious.

It wasn't the kindest hope, but she was an avenging angel at heart, so she let thoughts like those slide so long as they didn't blend into her actual behavior.

The spiral staircase up the tower was narrow, and while Bloom considered just flying and meeting them at the top, she supposed that show of power wouldn't sit well with the North Wind witch mayor. So she followed Clifford, taking up the rear of their small group.

When she stepped out into the open air again, she was grateful to be free of the confined space. It wasn't that she was claustrophobic, but it did make her antsy whenever she lacked the necessary room to spread her wings.

A dozen bells dangled in a spiral pattern from the center of the roof, and below them a yawning circular cavern down into darkness. Sunlight illuminated everything in this portion of the tower, and Bloom looked around, taking in the three-sixty views of Eastwind, obscured only by the pillars at each corner of the square tower holding up the domed ceiling.

The bells ranged noticeably in size, with the smallest perhaps a foot and a half tall and the largest easily four feet larger than Bloom herself. That one hung in the middle of the bell cluster, and was presumably the one that rang each hour, deep and, given the circumstances, foreboding.

The mayor began prattling on about this history of the tower, as if Bloom herself hadn't been present back when it was first constructed. But perhaps it was for Ruby's benefit, so she let the mayor continue.

"While Charn is the oldest of the bells, Duna is the real gem." He pointed at the largest one in the center of the cluster. "That's the lovely sound you hear chiming out the hours at noon and midnight each day."

As he went on to explain the process by which goblins had forged Duna, Bloom caught Ruby's eye. The psychic showed no signs of interest in what the mayor was telling her. Instead, she nodded toward a bell in the middle of the size range, one the mayor hadn't assigned a specific name.

Bloom inspected it. Nothing stood out. What was Ruby seeing that she wasn't?

It wasn't until she let her eyes wander to the other bells that she noticed.

It was older than the rest.

"That one," Bloom said, cutting off the mayor as she strode forward and pointed to the bell in question.

The mayor shot her a sharp look that carried venom, but she didn't care.

"Is this one Charn?"

The mayor strolled over. "No. That's, let me see..." he pointed at a few in turn, no doubt running through some mnemonic to refresh his memory. "That one's Twilie, I believe. *That one* is Charm. I just explained that, but it seems you weren't paying attention."

"I was paying plenty of attention," Bloom shot back. "Charn is the oldest bell here, right?"

He blinked. "Yes."

"Then how come Twilie looks so much more ancient?"

She hid her pleasure when Mayor Periwinkle scurried over to inspect it and saw that she was correct.

"That *is* strange. We just had the bells cleaned and restored two weeks ago. Twilie shouldn't be in that rough of a condition."

Bloom's eyes quickly found Ruby's.

"What does that entail, cleaning and restoring the bells?" Bloom asked.

"Oh, just someone coming up here, removing the bells one-by-one, filling in any cracks or damage, polishing them, and then putting them back on their hooks. The High Council makes sure it's done every few years."

"And who actually performs the work?"

He shrugged. "The lowest bidder for the project."

Of course.

"And who was the lowest bidder on it this time around?"

He pulled off his glasses and wiped them off on the sleeve of his suit. "Oh, I'm not really sure. It's not extremely technical work. You just have to have a tuning fork and an ear for tonality to make sure the bells aren't altered through the process."

"You don't know who was hired?" Bloom both could and couldn't believe the incompetency of Petrov Periwinkle.

He bristled. "I'm sure the Parchment Catacombs have the receipt for services somewhere."

"I'm sure they don't," Ruby muttered.

The mayor clearly heard her and shoved his glasses back onto his nose to give her a proper glare, but before he could say anything, Bloom jumped in again. "You should ask for a refund, Mayor. Whoever it was that performed the service completely skipped this bell, both polishing it *and* repairing it." While no chunks of it were missing that she could see, a few hairline fractures were easily visible down the side of it. "Did you speak with the hired labor at all?"

"Of course not," he snapped. "I have an assistant for that."

"I hope you pay her well."

"Oh, I do." He seemed to realize the trap he'd just walked into and tried to backtrack. "I mean, a reasonable amount. Not anything exorbitant that would take away from other budgets."

Clifford, who had been glued to Ruby's side since they'd ascended the stairs, stepped toward the bell, as close as he could get, and sniffed it. After a moment, Ruby's head tilted slightly, and she patted the hellhound on the head.

He had something. Some scent. Well, thank Heaven for that.

"Ruby, you have any questions for the mayor?"

"Oh, plenty. But none regarding the case at hand." The Fifth Wind smiled innocently, and a deep crease formed between Periwinkle's brows.

They left the bell tower then, and Bloom thanked the mayor for his valuable time once they reached the bottom and were back in the fresh air.

"If you can find out anything about who the contract labor was, please let me know."

"You think this has something to do with the two elves jumping?" he said.

"Don't you?"

He shrugged. "Couldn't say. To me, it just seems like

a boring case of two elves who have it all simply losing the will to live."

Bloom nodded along. "Yep. That's why I'm the sheriff and you aren't, sir." She turned to Ruby. "Come. I think we have quite a bit to discuss."

The Fifth Wind bowed her head. "I'll put on a kettle."

Chapter Twenty-One

"He recognized the scent, didn't he?" Sheriff Bloom asked as she sipped a strong black blend in Ruby's parlor.

Ruby had been thinking about that since Clifford had first told her about it. It just about seemed to tie the whole thing up with a pretty bow.

But not quite.

"He did," she replied, sitting opposite the sheriff at the round parlor table.

"And whose was it?" Bloom was clearly trying not to act impatient, but Ruby knew her too well. And why wouldn't she be impatient? Ruby herself was impatient to get this whole thing wrapped up. Could there be other elves at risk?

Perhaps only if there was an encore performance of the play. But three seemed to be the magic number this time.

"He can't tell definitively. But he recognized it from the room at the Ram's Head Inn." She crossed her legs and leaned back in her chair, cradling the steaming mug in her hands. "Whoever they hired to maintain the bells this time around was in that hotel room."

"Bitania?"

"That would certainly be my guess."

Bloom fell silent, and Ruby took the brief opportunity to let her mind drift. Time like this was precious. Did kids in Eastwind have enough time to sit a think? That seemed to her to be the only way to become a morally solid person, learning to think for oneself.

"Care to lay the whole thing out for me?" Bloom asked. "I feel like I might be missing a few pieces you have tucked away."

"It would be my pleasure." She sat up straighter, trying to locate the starting point of a thread. "That bell. The one Periwinkle called Twilie. I believe it's the root of Bron Danann's death, Dalora Greyborn's attempted death, and Magnus Taerwyn's outright creepy kitchen redecoration. I also believe it's the root of the attack in my bedroom. Moreover, I don't believe it's Twilie at all."

Bloom nodded. "That's what I was thinking, too."

"Where the bell came from and how long it's been there, I can only speculate."

"Oh, please do. Speculate away." Bloom kicked out her boots, crossing one foot over the other and settled in with the teacup cradled between both hands.

"Thank you. I don't mind if I do." Ruby grinned. "As for the *how long*, I believe that Bitania brought it with her into town only a couple of weeks ago. She must have been scouting Eastwind for a while and learned of the upcoming maintenance. Perhaps she'd been keeping an eye on it for years, since the last time they serviced the bells. How she originally learned of that routine, I can't even begin to guess. The possibilities are too vast. But one thing must be true: she was the lowest bidder on the work and was therefore allowed to enter the bell tower to conduct the maintenance. And that is when she switched Twilie with the one she brought. Which leads me to the *where* of it. I believe she brought the bell with her from Fallia itself."

Bloom nodded. "All this holds up. And I see where you're going with this, I think."

"I'm sure you do. Because besides the gross custom's violation of bringing the imposter Twilie in without notifying anyone, I believe the bell itself contained an illegal hitchhiker. The spirit of one Queen Naifa."

Bloom set down her cup. "See, that's where you lose me. It seems like a bit of a jump to say not only is the bell itself haunted, which I could buy if prompted, but that the winged entity that haunts it is specifically Queen Naifa."

Ruby nodded solemnly. "Then maybe it would help assuage your skepticism if I told you that the Queen Naifa depicted in the Rambling Mummers' production is, in fact, Queen Naifa *the Fifth*.."

Bloom's eyes opened wide. "Ah, now we're talking. When did you learn about that?"

"Yesterday. Stella Lytefoot was treating some minor bruising from the strangling and we got to talking."

Bloom leaned forward. "Looks like whatever she did worked. And if she's your source for that information, I'll take it to be fact."

"There is a slight chance the spirit is, say, the former queen's lover or some such," Ruby conceded. "I have considered that option, but the degree of power I've experienced firsthand speaks to two things: the entity was a powerful one *before* death, and after death, she is a *vengeful* one. And not your average vengeance. I believe her to be fueled with the kind of vengeance only one who has been both terribly betrayed and allowed to believe herself the most important person in the world could possess."

Bloom said, "Too true. Queens don't ascend to the throne without being raised to believe they're more important than the average peasant."

"Definitely not. The ego is a powerful force. And a destructive one."

"Why the elves, though?" Bloom asked. "Why Bron, Dalora, and Magnus?"

Ruby sucked in air like she'd stubbed a toe. "That I don't actually know." That was the *almost* in her theory being *almost* complete.

Bloom grinned. "I have a pretty good guess."

"Ooh! I do love your theories," she replied, grabbing the kettle and pouring herself another cup before topping off the sheriff. "They're always full of poetic justice."

"And this one is no different," Bloom replied. "How closely did you watch the play?"

"As closely as someone with no tolerance for theater and a big, sexy werebear next to her could."

"So not very closely."

"No, I wouldn't say so."

Bloom nodded. "On stage, the queen's three guards were fairies."

"They were all fairies."

"Correct. But the three protecting her were fairies *playing elves.*"

Ruby felt her mouth fall open before she could stop it. Of course. She'd missed that bit. She'd been sure to pay attention to the actual scene in the tower, but she'd missed the lead-up to it.

"Three elves?"

Bloom nodded. "Apparently, it was traditional in Fallia for elves, being the biggest and strongest of the fae, to train as guard for the queen herself. Of course, that tradition was quickly dropped after the events depicted in the play took place."

"And how long ago did the events depicted in the play take place?"

Bloom rubbed her chin and she thought.

Ah, yes, thought Ruby, there was that little bit of drama from her earlier days in Heaven.

"Oh, I'd say it all took place right before three elves showed up in Eastwind requesting Liberty's assistance in creating a totally invisible avenue on which no one who might want to murder them could find them."

"Sounds about right. And why noon? Why midnight?"

Bloom narrowed her eyes. "Surely you've figured that out as well."

And now Ruby, who'd been so pleased with herself only moment before, was starting to feel genuinely silly. "You know but you're not going to tell me? Okay, fine. I'll do it myself."

She fell silent, staring at the serene burgundy surface of her tea. Her Insight quickly perked up when summoned and pointed her back toward the Pixie Mixie. The bell. When it rang...

She had it.

"Noon and midnight are the only times when the clock tower plays the entire lead in before chiming the hours. The spirit is awakened whenever the imposter of Twilie is rung."

Bloom shrugged a shoulder. "That's my guess, at least."

Ruby considered it for another moment. "But she must return at some point, yes? She's not free to roam around for the rest of the day."

"Attached to the sound perhaps?"

"That'll do."

"Three guards, three shows," Bloom said, staring absently at one of the warding baubles above Ruby's head. "Does that mean the town has nothing to worry about? That the danger for Dalora and Magnus will pass once the Rambling Mummers' ramble their way out of town?"

"Only if they take that bell with them," Ruby supposed. "It seems like the bell itself was the cause of all the trouble. But then why bother with the play?" She continued, talking it out aloud. "If Bitania could have just as easily slipped into Eastwind, replaced the bell, and let it do the damage, why risk all the eyes on them by performing during the planned attacks?" She shook her head. "It doesn't make sense."

"Firstly," Bloom said, "you're expecting the behavior of professional actors to make sense." At Ruby's surprised look, she said, "What? I can enjoy the theater and also accept that it's full of strange people." She sighed. "Perhaps Bitania and whoever else might have been complicit liked the poetry of it all. Or maybe Bitania wanted an excuse to be there to see it happen."

"Or maybe..." Ruby began, letting that quote surface once again.

The play's the thing...

"Maybe she knew that a theatrical performance of the murder they committed would pique their interest. It's not a bad lure, you know. They murder their queen, flee, and then centuries later, a traveling band of players is performing the very act. I know I'd be interested in seeing how it was all presented. And my guilty conscience might drive me there as well. I might feel like I deserved to sit and watch what I'd done, to confront it."

Bloom nodded. "That would make the play a powerful lure to make sure at least one of them was within a reasonable distance of the clock tower and could fall from the top."

"Like Queen Naifa the Fifth was tossed from her tower, yes." She shook her head, narrowing her eyes at the angel. "You really are a dramatic bunch. The flare for drama is just too rich for my blood."

"In this case, it's a little too rich for mine as well."

As Bloom took another long sip of tea, Ruby said, "They'll be leaving either today or tomorrow, won't they? Now that the last curtain has fallen."

Bloom swallowed and shook her head. "And I don't have a good feeling about the entire troop making it out of Eastwind. I have this funny feeling they're about to lose their troop leader."

Ruby arched an eyebrow. "Lose her to?"

"Justice."

Ruby laughed. "Oh, Gabby. You must have made a fine thespian. But while it is a beautiful story we've spun here, it's still only a story. We have very little evidence. How do you plan on apprehending her lawfully?"

"The old-fashioned way. We get her to confess."

The Fifth Wind arched an eyebrow. "We? Sounds like you already have a plan."

Bloom waved her off. "Please. I always have a plan. That's why I'm sheriff. Now would you be so kind as to bring me a piece of parchment and something a pen? The murdered Queen Naifa has a letter to write."

Chapter Twenty-Two

"All I want is for you to admit that you love this part of the job," Clifford said.

They were in the top of the clocktower, surrounded by darkness. The time was eleven fifty-seven P.M.

"What part," Ruby replied, *"staying up past my bedtime?"*

"No. The danger."

"I don't know why you seem so keen on me admitting that."

"Because the sooner you stop pretending it's an imposition, the sooner you can start truly enjoying it."

"Ah, so you're merely looking out for my happiness."

"Someone has to."

Ruby rolled her eyes and was glad it was too dark for Clifford to notice.

Would Bitania respond to the summons from her queen? There were a lot of possible flaws in their plan. For one, they had no idea what the fairy queen's handwriting looked like. Would Bitania know? One of the things they hadn't been able to speculate on was why the fairy was so set on vengeance. Had she known the queen personally? Or was she simply a fanatic? And if she'd known the queen, would she be able to tell the letter was a fake? Could she remember handwriting after so long a time?

They had attempted to compensate for that by explaining in the letter that she was possessing another body to write the letter and send it.

But there was one obvious flaw in that, too: *when* would she have written it?

As far as they were aware, the fairy queen only left the confines of her bell each time it rang, and that was only at noon and midnight. Then she was recalled to it as the sound faded, not to emerge again until the next toll.

Ruby's hope was that Bitania was at least moderately insane, which wasn't too much of a shot in the dark for an actor. If the fairy had delusions of grandeur, which was almost a guarantee, the flattery they'd included in the letter might be enough to make her forget all about that small technicality.

But the bell was about to ring again. And Ruby was certain that she would come face to face with the entity that tried to strangle her to death when that happened.

Maybe Clifford was right. Maybe she did enjoy the danger. It certainly made her feel more alert than usual. And being this alert, feeling her heart flutter in her chest, was a novelty that increased year by year.

Any minute now. Literally.

She walked carefully to the edge of the tower, making sure not to get too close to the hole in the center as she did. Bracing herself on one of the four stone beams, she gazed over the edge to make sure her backup was still waiting below.

Sheriff Bloom was almost impossible to spot in the shadows. If Ruby hadn't been looking, she wouldn't have noticed her.

Well, that was good. If things really went amiss, it was comforting to know there was a crime-fighting immortal being from Heaven who had her back.

"You thinking about jumping?" came a gruff voice behind her. "I wouldn't suggest it."

Perhaps she was more tightly wound than she had realized, because the sudden sound made her jump half a foot into the air. She clutched the stone column with both hands to make sure she didn't lose her balance and topple.

Once she was stable, she turned around to face the source of the voice.

Clifford was already growling, hackles up, at the hovering fairy.

But it wasn't Bitania.

She recognized his turquoise wings immediately and tried to recall his name. Willford? Wendel? Ah! Welling. That was it. The one Bitania had carelessly shoved off the chair in the hotel room.

"Call off the hound," he said. "I just want to talk."

Ruby asked her familiar to give the fairy a little space, and he did as he was told, but his hackles remained raised.

The fairy's wings beat rapidly as he remained on eye level with her, perhaps only ten feet away.

She shouldn't have moved so close to the edge. She had no room to retreat now if she needed.

"I thought," she began, "it was Bitania."

He grinned, and as he did so, the moonlight glinted off his teeth—what he had left of them, at least. Two large gaps where some were missing caught her eye like dangerous black wells with no bottom. "I know you did. And that, among other things, is how I knew the letter wasn't from Queen Naifa."

"I'm surprised you knew about the letter at all, then. It wasn't addressed to you."

He scoffed. "She thought it was a secret admirer role-playing the queen. Very *fancy*. She decided to show it around so we all could revel in how special she was for being singled out." He scowled. "She's not special. She thinks this is all just a performance. She wasn't there during the revolution." He fluttered a foot closer. "But I was. After the guards killed the queen, they threw her body from the tower. I was the one who found it." He fluttered closer still, his voice deepening with malice. "We were lovers. I'd long had my suspicions about those elves, but she insisted they were the strongest and the best suited for the job. She didn't see their looks of contempt behind her back. Elvenkind couldn't stand a fairy holding the highest honor in the realm. They thought it should have been them. I told her. I *told* her."

Ruby inched to her left. She wasn't in a position to move away from the edge, but she could at least get her back up against the stone pillar so she couldn't be pushed or lose her balance and fall.

Welling didn't seem to notice. He was lost in his memory, that was easy enough to see. "So when I heard they'd taken her to the tower to protect her from the rebels, I flew there immediately, despite the danger of crossing the army's line. But... I was too late. Her wings were broken, and she was white as a ghost, crumpled in a heap at the base of the tower like a discarded sack of trash."

And then the bells began to ring.

Chapter Twenty-Three

It happened as soon as the ancient bell was struck. The spirit of Queen Naifa leaped free and appeared beside Welling.

"My love," he breathed, moving toward her.

But she had eyes only for Ruby. And boy, were those eyes full of murder.

"How dare you try to stop me. I've waited centuries for this revenge. It doesn't involve you, witch!"

Ruby shrugged. "Agree to disagree."

The queen shot forward, barreling toward her.

Normally, a spirit rushing her wouldn't have been too concerning. After all, they went through objects, and she'd long since learned how to avoid an unwanted possession.

But this one was different. The power of the fairy queen was different. She'd experienced that firsthand. This one could muster the energy to affect physical objects; namely, strangle them.

Good thing Ruby kept another physical object by her side that was equally tricky to mess with...

Clifford sprang, jaws snapping, taking the impact of the queen without so much as a flinch.

He might have already outlived the lifespan of the average hellhound, but he had by no means slowed down in his advanced years. Clifford could move quick when he needed to. And this was one of those times when he needed to.

The spirit tried to shoot past him again, but he moved and blocked her once more.

On her third charge, though, she went straight through him. She'd figured out the trick.

"Fangs and claws!" Ruby yelped, ducking right as the spirit solidified and dove for her. The stone right behind where Ruby's head had been exploded, raining fragments down into her hair.

Ruby opened her eyes, which she'd close reflexively as she flinched, and saw the queen making another charge.

But the snicker-snack of Clifford's teeth marked the end of that. Because when Naifa had made herself material again in hopes of punishing the witch, she'd also left herself vulnerable to an attack from the familiar. He grabbed one of her ghostly feet and flung her back toward Welling, who was watching with slack-jawed admiration.

The queen yelled her frustration. And then she disappeared.

Right into Welling.

The largest bell, Duna, rang in the first of twelve hours.

And then Queen Naifa's words issue from Welling's

lips. "Will your hellhound kill him? Can you justify that act?"

Doooom...

"If you made him attack me," Ruby said, "I can't think of a more justified reason. But you wouldn't do that, would you? You loved him." She considered inching away from the pillar again, but with the edge of the tower behind her and the yawning chasm of the bells ahead of her, she decided it safer to simply keep her back against something solid.

Doooom...

"He was a lover," the fairy queen replied. "But I didn't love him."

Wow. Poor Welling. What a way to find out. For his sake, Ruby hoped he'd been pushed too deep into the recesses of his own mind to make room for her spirit that he wouldn't remember that unfortunate confession. Although, wait. He'd been the instigator in all this. Well, then it served him right!

"But he's served you well," she said, stalling, hoping Sheriff Bloom could hear some of the scuffle amidst the ear-numbing sound of the bells and might deign to join them and save the day. If not, she only need hold off the brutal tyrant until the end of the bells. "He got you here so you could have—"

Doooom...

"—your revenge."

"He was the one who trapped my soul in the bell in the first place! It was his revenge he wanted, not mine."

Doooom...

"And he's failed at it," she continued. "I would be doing him a favor by killing him."

Doooom...

Ruby's objective tonight wasn't merely to survive a few minutes in the ring with a deranged entity. She'd come to put an end to things without allowing any more deaths. And Welling's odds of survival were looking slimmer with each word that was forced through his hijacked mouth.

She could try to exorcise him, but not from this distance. If she could lay a hand on him, she might be able to banish the queen once and for all...

Doooom...

Could she do it quickly enough to avoid injury?

But the question became moot the instant Welling sprinted for the edge of the tower.

He was trying to escape, to fly off and—

But the fairy never spread his turquoise wings. Instead, he ran off the side and dropped like a rock.

Doooom...

"No!" Ruby shouted, reaching out.

Clifford had made a lung for him as well, trying to snatch the fairy back as soon as he'd realized what Naifa had in store for her former lover. But Clifford, no matter how agile, never stood a chance.

Doooom...

Then suddenly, Queen Naifa was back, hovering just by the bells, her intense glow lighting up the night.

But Ruby was ready for her now. She hadn't wanted it to come to this, but it was the only viable option to end this once and for all. The deadly queen would never return to that bell. It was time for her to go.

Ruby closed her eyes, opened her arms, and summoned the fairy spirit inside of her.

The invitation was readily accepted.

Cliff had her arms and legs pinned to the ground in a heartbeat, keeping the queen from taking over her body and injuring her in the time it took to finish the banishment.

You're a fool, the spirit spoke inside her head.

Then suddenly they were somewhere else. No longer surrounded by the unforgiving stone of Fallia's Eye, Ruby had brought them to the in-between place. A place in her mind she'd crafted meticulously, where she could reach out to wandering spirits at will.

Or bring a restless one who had overstayed her welcome.

They were on Ruby's turf now.

Over years of practice, Ruby had created this spot from memories of her life long ago, before she came to Eastwind. And now she stood in the shamrock-green grass by the sparkling pond, the perpetual sunset ahead of her...

And the vengeful spirit beside her. The fairy no longer looked like a spirit, though. She had her color back, and her substance.

After a moment of shock from finding herself in this incongruously peaceful setting, the queen lunged at the witch in whose head she now resided.

That was all Ruby needed. Her age was of no consequence here. In this in-between place, she was ageless. Her movement was limited only by her imagination, but she'd never had a shortage of that. No one who read as much fiction as she did could be lacking in that department.

She ducked, and as Naifa flew over her, she grabbed the fairy's hands. It was all the contact she needed.

She blasted her energy outward through the connection. The queen shuddered then screamed as she was ripped apart, torn into smaller and smaller pieces until each bit of her became no larger than a speck of spring pollen and blew away on the wind.

Ruby collapsed onto her back, panting in the grass, gazing up at a blue sky.

Wait, no. *She* wasn't panting. She didn't need to pant. She couldn't be physically exhausted here.

But someone was definitely panting.

Ruby opened her eyes and found herself staring into her familiar's hairy face. His stifling breath blasted her with each of his heavy, nervous pants.

"You can get off me now, Cliff," she said politely.

He did, and she was glad to get a lungful of fresh air following it. She crawled to her feet and dusted herself off. "Thanks." Then she gave him the head scratch he deserved.

"Any time."

A gust of wind made her turn, and she found Bloom beating her wings in long strokes as she landed at the tower's edge. "You okay?"

Ruby smiled pleasantly and tried to pat her hair back into submission. "Totally. Everything is fine here. Nothing at all strange or dangerous. What about Welling?"

Bloom nodded toward the edge and Ruby, cautiously, glanced over.

The fairy was hogtied on the ground, shining gold

ropes casting a soft glow over him. His wings were bound as well. He wasn't going anywhere.

"I flew up to check on you when I heard the shouting, but suddenly a fairy was falling from the sky, and I became slightly preoccupied tending to him." She paused. "It wasn't Bitania."

"Nope. We were both wrong."

Bloom frowned, unconcerned. "I'd say our wrong was still pretty right."

"It worked out in the end, at least."

Bloom nodded. "You want a lift down?"

Ruby opened her mouth to decline, but her heart was still racing in her chest, craving more adrenaline. She'd crash later, maybe even sleep until noon. Oh! What an indulgence! "Why not?" she said.

Bloom scooped Ruby into her arms and leaped off the side of the tower.

There seemed to be a lot of that lately. Too much.

But with any luck, Ruby thought, this would be the last of it.

Epilogue

Ruby awoke to bright sunlight streaming through a small crack in her thick curtains. What time was it? Cliff probably needed to use the bathroom outside.

She blinked and sat up, holding the quilt close to her.

Her familiar was still snoozing on his bed, emitting light, rhythmic snores.

She looked at the clock. It was nearly eleven in the morning.

She'd crawled into bed after one that morning, after having settled on a plan with Bloom for wrapping up the loose ends of the case. The angel had insisted she could take it from there and that Ruby would be smart to go home. And besides, Bloom didn't need to sleep. She only preferred a few hours of deep meditation to process things each day, but it was by no means mandatory for her survival. Obviously.

Ten hours of sleep, Ruby had enjoyed. What was she, a teenager?

If only, she thought sleepily, before remembering

she'd hated her teen years. So much excess angst, so little wisdom. No, forty-six was a much more pleasant age, all creaky joints and unexpected internal temperature fluctuations aside. Slightly less angst, and slightly more wisdom.

The possession was the likely culprit for that morning's long doze. Spiritual battle always took it out of her.

She glanced at Clifford again. Watching him sleep only made her want to go back to bed. Any why not? She'd earned it.

But then she remembered. She had plans. Once Bloom had left her cottage the previous afternoon, Ruby had arranged to meet with Zax up at Treetop Lodge on Fluke Mountain for lunch to make up for her sudden departure from the Emporium the day before.

The thought of it made her groan.

Wait, why had she groaned? She liked Zax.

She chalked it up to the exhaustion.

After pulling on a warm robe and her favorite slippers, she fixed herself a light breakfast and downed the strongest tea she had, wishing she had some coffee instead. Sure, the stuff made her a bit blunt and wired, but it was also the perfect elixir to help her recover from a night like the one she'd just had.

She checked the clock. She was supposed to be at the restaurant in fifteen minutes. She was hardly ready, not even properly dressed, and the walk alone took her twenty unless she was really hustling. But she was in no condition to hustle. Not this morning.

It all seemed like a lot of effort. Maybe she ought to send an owl his way asking to relocate it somewhere nearer to her house or push back the time. That wasn't asking too much.

But still, it felt like more effort than she had to give today. He would want to talk about the case, and she would feel inclined to fill him in, rehashing events she hadn't yet wrapped her own head around.

It wasn't his fault, of course. She would have asked the same questions if their positions had been switched.

Zax was a wonderful man and good company.

And yet...

She turned to Clifford, who had relocated with her downstairs only to fall right back to sleep belly-up on the rug by the fireplace. "What do you think about a meat pie?"

His head jerked then he flopped onto his side. "*I think yes. Same as always.*"

She nodded. It was settled then. But first, she had to write two letters. The first was to Zax. It said, "*Feeling under the weather today. Afraid I have to cancel. Sorry about the short notice. I hope you treat yourself to a delicious meal regardless.*"

And then the second letter: "*A New Leaf at noon? I could go for a coffee.*"

She sent both of them off, and by the time she'd cleaned her breakfast dishes and changed clothes, she had two replies waiting in her inbox below the owl's perch. The first was from Zax.

She unfolded it and read, "*I heard you had a big night. Rest up. We'll enjoy a steak together soon.*"

Of course. Leave it to him to be unnaturally understanding. He *was* a good man. She set that slip of parchment aside and unrolled the second response:

"Perfect. I could use a chat with the bluntest witch in Eastwind."

Ruby grinned.

"Come, Cliff." She patted her thigh and he met her at the door. "We have a coffee date."

* * *

The bell above the entrance to the tearoom chimed airily as Ruby held the door open for Clifford. Moving from sunshine to the dim space made her pause as her eyes adjusted.

Harvey Hardtime's face was the first one she spotted, mostly because she knew exactly where to find him behind the counter.

"Usual?" he called.

"No. Coffee, please."

He lifted his eyebrows in apparent astonishment. "You must've had an even crazier Saturday night than I did."

"For your sake, I hope so."

She scanned the room and located her date without any trouble. Yes, these plans suited her much better than the previous ones.

Clifford marched straight to the hellhound bed in the corner and fell asleep. She couldn't blame him. He wasn't a fan of coffee or tea, so he had no crutches after long nights.

Gabby Bloom looked up from a book as Ruby reached the table. "Ah, there you are. I was worried you'd simply go back to bed and skip out."

Ruby went with honesty. "I almost did." She looked down at the sheriff's book. "What you reading?"

Bloom flashed the front. *The Lonely Vampire Widower*. There was no mistaking the genre once Ruby glimpsed the pale, shirtless man on the cover. Perhaps in her earlier years she would have blushed or scoffed at such a thing. But no more. She'd decidedly dropped that taboo as soon as she'd discovered how pleasantly one could while away the afternoon in a comfortable chair by the fire with such a companion as was found between those covers.

"Romance?" she said, lowering herself into her chair. "I didn't peg you as the type."

"Yeah, well," Bloom said evasively, "maybe you're rubbing off on me."

"All the better for you. That's a good one."

"You've read it?"

"Three times."

Bloom held up a palm. "Don't spoil the ending."

Ruby rolled her eyes. "Spoil it? It's a romance. You know how it ends."

"The main characters end up together. I know, I know. But don't tell me *how* it happens."

Ruby gasped dramatically, hand to her heart. "I wouldn't *dream* of it."

Harvey set a giant mug of coffee on the table in front of her. "No offense," he said, "but you looked like you could use a large one."

"None taken... so long as you get my familiar here your freshest meat pie."

Harvey laughed. "Already heating it in the oven."

Ruby took a tiny sip of her coffee. It was still too hot to drink in earnest, but the smell alone invigorated her.

As Bloom marked her page with a silky silver ribbon and set the book aside, Ruby said, "Loose ends tied up?"

"For now. Welling is in jail awaiting his trial. I checked in on Dalora and Magnus this morning, too, let them know the worst was over and they could relax."

"Are you going to arrest them?" She lowered her voice. "After all, they did murder a monarch."

Bloom waved it off. "Out of my jurisdiction. And it was hundreds of years ago. I have enough to handle in Eastwind *now*."

"Did they tell you why they murdered her?"

Bloom shrugged. "Sure, but take it with a grain of salt, you know? They said she'd been systematically murdering the leaders of the other fae races. Growing paranoid, et cetera, et cetera."

"You don't believe them?"

"You can't believe anything people say about something that happened that long ago. Everyone wears down their memory over time, smoothing the rough edges of their own actions and motivations. It's possible they're telling the truth. But one thing is certain: I don't care. As long as they're not going to cause problems around here, they can stay cloistered up in Tearnanock Estates all they want. Like I said, out of my jurisdiction." She held up her hands to show how done she was with it.

"Sounds like you have it all tied up, then."

Bloom grinned. "Not yet. I still have one important thing left to do."

"And that is?"

"I have to pay a visit to the High Council and let

them know Mayor Periwinkle was responsible for hiring a lunatic for the sake of saving a copper or two."

"Ooh..." Ruby said. "Who needs to read romance when you have real life fantasies like that to look forward to?"

Bloom laughed, and it was a glorious thing to behold. The weight of the very air around them seemed to lift whenever it happened.

Already feeling more energized, Ruby ventured another sip of her coffee. The angel watched her closely and then said, "Let me know when you're feeling properly caffeinated."

Uh-oh. Ruby recognized that tone. "Okay, why?" She cocked her head to the side, eying the sheriff with suspicion.

"Because" said Bloom, reclining in her seat and slinging an arm over the back of the chair, "I have another case I could use your help on."

The End of Book 2
Turn the page for more Ruby True...

VAMPIRE'S IRE
A Ruby True Magical Mystery 3

Fifth Wind witch Ruby True wants to be left alone with a good book to heal an aching heart. But when an unidentified vampire is found dead in Veris Bluffs Asylum, the sheriff wrangles her into applying her gifts for hire.

But when Ruby discovers the victim's lingering spirit, something no vampire is reported to have, there may be only one man who can answer their many questions. Unfortunately, he's the last person whose word she would trust...

Will Ruby get the the heart of the murder before her broken heart gets the best of her?

Read Vampire's Ire now:

www.eastwindwitches.com/ruby3

GET AN EXCLUSIVE EASTWIND WITCHES BOOK - FREE!

The Missing Motive follows a murder that takes place two years before Nora arrives in Eastwind.

With Sheriff Bloom by her side, Ruby True attempts to figure out who killed the insufferable druid who has taken up residence in her home.

Enjoy the divine duo of True and Bloom, and visit some of your favorite Eastwind townsfolk in this humorous caper!

This book is only available to members of the Cozy Coven, Nova Nelson's reader group.

Click the link below to join and claim your book:

Join the Cozy Coven

Go to www.cozycoven.com

About the Author

Nova Nelson grew up on a steady diet of Agatha Christie novels. She loves the mind candy of cozy mysteries and has been weaving paranormal tales since she first learned handwriting. Those two loves meet in her Eastwind Witches series, and it's about time, if she does say so herself.

When she's not busy writing, she enjoys long walks with her strong-willed dogs and eating breakfast for dinner.

Say hello:
nova@novanelson.com

www.ingramcontent.com/pod-product-compliance
Lightning Source LLC
Chambersburg PA
CBHW061621100726
47898CB00002B/759